"Kiss me, Ronnie,"

Blake said, his voice rough.

"This is crazy," she sighed.

"We have to make people believe I'm the only man in the world you want."

"I think you're taking this a little far," she said, but slipped her arms around his neck just the same.

He wanted a convincing performance, so she'd give him one. "Just don't expect a declaration of love, Detective."

She sucked in a sharp breath when his warm lips skirted along her jaw to her throat. She tipped her head back, not because what he was doing felt wonderfully delicious, but to provide a convincing performance.

Uh-huh. Sure, her conscience taunted.

Ronnie gave in to the desire by pressing her fingers against the back of his neck, urging his mouth over hers. He tasted sweet, hard and hot. She never wanted it to end.

"Convincing enough for you?" she asked, surprised by the strength in her voice.

"Yeah," he muttered with roughness in his tone. "Plenty."

"Good." She lifted he
a satisfied expression
she felt anything bu
devil for an icy shov

Dear Reader,

Every so often a secondary character emerges that catches a writer's eye, and detective Blake Hammond was one such character. I met Blake when I was writing *Flirting with Danger* (#708), and for two years he sat in the back of my mind just waiting for the right woman to come along. When sassy DEA Agent Veronica Carmichael appeared, we both knew she was "the one."

This is one story that couldn't have been told without the assistance of a few important people. I'd like to offer a very special thank-you to Officer Darrell Drouin of the East Hartford Police Department for answering all of my questions on jurisdiction and interdepartmental procedures. A big thank-you to the Renville County Sheriff's Department, and especially to Renville County Deputy Sheriff Marlyn Eklund who always offers a smile when answering even my most bizarre "what if" questions as they relate to inner workings of the criminal element. You guys are the best!

I'd love to hear what you think of Blake and Veronica's romance. You can write to me by e-mail at jamie@jamiedenton.net or to P.O. Box 224, Mohall, ND 58761.

Warmest regards,

Jamie Denton

Books by Jamie Denton

UNDER THE COVERS
Jamie Denton

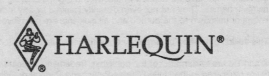

HARLEQUIN®

TORONTO • NEW YORK • LONDON
AMSTERDAM • PARIS • SYDNEY • HAMBURG
STOCKHOLM • ATHENS • TOKYO • MILAN • MADRID
PRAGUE • WARSAW • BUDAPEST • AUCKLAND

For Kane, Katelyn and Jadyn
This one is for you my little angels.

ISBN 0-373-25957-3

UNDER THE COVERS

Copyright © 2001 by Jamie Ann Denton.

This edition published by arrangement with Harlequin Books S.A.

® and TM are trademarks of the publisher. Trademarks indicated with
® are registered in the United States Patent and Trademark Office, the
Canadian Trade Marks Office and in other countries.

Visit us at www.eHarlequin.com

Printed in U.S.A.

1

EXHAUSTED, Detective Blake Hammond dropped into the worn leather chair, leaned back and propped his polished brown loafers on the edge of the gray metal desk. He glanced at the clock hanging on the far wall and managed a tired grin, anxious to wrap up the long unproductive night of surveillance. In less than twelve hours he'd be on a 747 to the Hawaiian Islands. The most strenuous item on his agenda consisted of downing a variety of fruity rum drinks, while appreciating the view of sunbathing beauties intent on deepening their tans under the warm tropical sunshine.

Life was good, and bound to be an improvement over the last month, which had been filled with long hours that hadn't garnered a solid arrest. For the past two weeks, he'd been convinced the lead from a snitch was a dead end. A series of robberies in Los Angeles's high-rent district had the lieutenant demanding a bust, but so far, Blake and his new partner, Lucas Stone, had turned up nothing. The robberies were clean, no forced entry and not a single print or scrap of evidence left by the perps.

"You don't have to gloat, Hammond." Luke tossed a thin file near Blake's feet. "It's depressing to the rest of us grunts left behind to deal with the criminal element."

"I've earned the right to gloat," Blake said with a chuckle, swinging his feet to the floor. "I haven't had a vacation in over three years. For the next fourteen days the only surveillance I'm planning has to do with curvy, suntanned, string-bikini-clad bodies glistening with coconut-scented oil."

Luke dropped into the chair behind the desk adjacent to Blake's. "Great," he grumbled, reaching for the phone after shoving a lock of sandy-brown hair off his forehead. "I'm stuck partnering that blowhard bore, Pearson, while you're scoping beach-bound Bettys. There's just something unfair about that."

"You know what they say about life being fair," Blake said without an ounce of remorse, glancing up as Lieutenant Forbes came out of his office.

"Hammond. A minute," Forbes barked. His salt-and-pepper eyebrows were pulled into a heavy frown Blake was certain didn't bode well.

Blake shot a look in his partner's direction. Luke shrugged and punched numbers into the telephone keypad.

"Close the door," Forbes ordered when Blake walked into the lieutenant's office. He perched on the edge of his desk while Blake propped his backside on the arm of the leather sofa that sat against the far wall.

"I'm canceling your vacation."

Blake came off the sofa. "No. You're not." Let Forbes write him up for insubordination. He needed a vacation before he made a serious, and costly, mistake. The previous week he'd gotten a little too rough with a suspect. He didn't want to think about what could've happened if Luke hadn't pulled him off the creep. Blake had been appalled by his own behavior. His usual calm and patience had slipped out of frustration, telling him loud and clear he was overdue for some much needed R and R, something he planned to rectify in the next twelve hours.

A tired cop made mistakes. An overworked cop was dangerous.

A frustrated cop was deadly.

"I haven't had time off in three years," Blake said, frowning. He stuffed his hands in the front pockets of his pressed khaki trousers and gave Forbes a hard look. "I'm tired, Lieutenant. I need a break."

Forbes crossed his arms over his barrel chest. "I know you need a vacation, Hammond. I wouldn't do this to you, but I don't have a choice. I need someone to go undercover with DEA."

"DEA? Oh, come on, Lieutenant. I'm not in the mood to be hassled by some government agent over petty jurisdictional issues. Give it to Stone. I'm tired."

"Stone's too involved in the uptown robbery. I need someone familiar to stay on that case. You're the only one free for the next couple of weeks."

"A couple of weeks somewhere warm and tropical, not holed up with an uptight, arrogant DEA agent."

"It'll be light duty."

Blake gave a harsh laugh. "Light duty? With the DEA involved? Yeah, and the CIA's adopted a kinder, gentler method of interrogation, too. Tell me another fairy tale, Lieutenant."

"I'm still your superior officer, Hammond," Forbes said in that cold-as-steel voice he'd perfected as a beat cop back in the glory days of the LAPD. "This is a special situation and you're needed."

Blake took a deep breath and attempted to summon his trademark calm and cool demeanor. He felt as if he was fighting a losing battle as the thought of handing in his shield played on the fringes of his mind. Just the fact that he even considered walking out was solid proof he needed to get away for a while. Good cops didn't make mistakes, or take their frustrations out on suspects. The role of good cop was as natural as breathing to him.

Lately he'd forgotten how to breathe.

"Is that an order, Lieutenant?" he asked, his voice filled with a composure that felt far too foreign to be realistic.

Forbes returned Blake's hard stare with one of his own. "Yeah, Hammond. It's an order."

Irritation climbed up Blake's spine and settled in his neck. He let out a long breath and rubbed at the tension. "Fine," he said after another deep breath that did little to ease his frustration. "My airline ticket's non-refundable. I want to be reimbursed." If the department was going to screw him out of a vacation, then they could damn well pay for the privilege, he thought irritably.

Forbes nodded sharply. "I'll see what I can do about it. This is coming from the brass upstairs, so it shouldn't be a problem. As soon as you've wrapped this assignment up, you can take off."

With nothing else to say, Blake dropped onto the edge of the sofa. He didn't like it, and the churning in his gut confirmed his suspicions. He despised being backed into a corner, but an order was an order which left him with no other option than to comply. "What am I getting into?"

Forbes circled the desk, opened a file and stood with his hands braced on the large desk. "This isn't just an L.A. problem," he said looking at Blake. "The word on the street is a new designer drug is hitting the West Coast. There are already reports that it's starting to show up in the Midwest and, we can assume, moving farther east."

"Colombians?" Blake asked. He was familiar with drug trafficking, as were all the detectives in Vice. Busting the bad guys, the small-timers and even the movers and shakers in the underworld was part of his everyday life. The only reason he and Luke had been stuck on the uptown robbery detail was that their snitch had refused to provide information to anyone other than Luke.

"Not this time," Forbes answered, shifting his attention to the open file. "According to Ronnie Carmichael, the agent you'll be working with, this new brand of synthetic coke is being smuggled into the States through Avalon."

Blake leaned forward, braced his elbows on his legs, and clasped his hands between his knees. "Catalina Island?" Interesting, he thought. Southern California's island retreat was more of a place for lovers and honeymooners than drug traffickers. "How are they getting it out?"

A knock at the door had Forbes moving around his desk. "DEA suspects it's being brought out by chopper or run out of Avalon Harbor on the launches," he said, reaching the door and resting his hand on the knob. "There are about twenty or more runs back and forth between Avalon and Long Beach Harbor per day."

"Which provides plenty of opportunity for movement," Blake surmised.

"Considering the Coast Guard has never paid a whole lot of attention to the water taxis, you're right."

"That could explain how the stuff's getting out of Avalon."

"That's what you're going to find out," Forbes said as he opened the door. "And stop."

Standing in the threshold was a woman. Not just any woman, but a breathtakingly beautiful one. Blake gazed into eyes a startling shade of brilliant turquoise and felt his heart slam into his ribs.

"I apologize for being late," she said quickly.

She shifted her attention to Forbes, and away from that instant spark of awareness Blake would bet his badge she'd felt, too. Not only did she have the softest, sweetest voice he'd ever heard with just a trace of a Southern accent he found sexy as sin, but the slight smile canting her lips caused an adorable dimple to wink at him. "Your L.A. interchange was a little more than I expected."

Forbes commanded her attention and ushered her into the room while Blake took advantage of her movements, allowing his gaze to travel the length of her. He had no idea who she was, but she had the kind of legs that made a man sit up and take notice, slender and shapely, like the rest of her. When it came to the appreciation of women, Blake considered himself an expert. And in his expert opinion, the curvaceous brunette was a vast improvement over the last department secretary. If this was the type of support staff personnel was placing in the detectives' bureau, he might just stop complaining about having to ride a desk for hours at a time to deal with the endless stream of paperwork.

Her sensible, low-heeled pumps clicked sharply on the linoleum as she crossed the small office space to the pair of mismatched chairs opposite Forbes's desk. Always the gentleman, Blake stood, hoping to gain an introduction to the petite dream come true.

A straight peach skirt reached just above her shapely knees and a soft, floral-print blouse brought out the intriguing color of her eyes. He usually liked his women tall, but he'd make an exception for the looker with a thick file tucked under her arm.

She glanced over her shoulder at him, and Blake flashed her his most winning smile. Delicately arched eyebrows rose briefly, and those turquoise eyes looked him up and down without showing the slightest hint of interest, curious or otherwise, before turning her attention back to the lieutenant.

Just as well, Blake thought, even if he didn't buy her

disinterest for a nanosecond. She more than piqued his interest, but she was off-limits since the department had a strict fraternization policy that applied to all law enforcement and support staff personnel.

"Blake," Forbes said, drawing his attention from her lethal legs. "This is Special Agent Veronica Carmichael, from the Drug Enforcement Agency. Ronnie will be your partner for the next couple of weeks."

Blake looked from the slight grin tugging his superior's lips to the lust-inspiring brunette and back again. *Ronny* was *Ronnie?*

"This is a practical joke, right?" he asked desperately.

No way was all that honey and sweetness an uptight, arrogant DEA agent. The few times he'd crossed paths with Drug Enforcement agents, they were hard-drinking, rough-talking, take-no-prisoners brick walls of solid muscle with a penchant for risking their thick, beefy necks. She didn't look as if she could withstand a brisk Santa Ana wind, let alone wrestle a whacked-out dust dealer to the ground.

"I assure you, Detective," she said, a flash of determination lining her delicate Southern accent. "I'm no joke."

"You're going to be my partner?" he asked carefully.

"I hope you don't have a problem taking orders from a woman," she said, a saccharine smile curving her lips.

"Taking orders?" he asked incredulously. "There

must be a page missing from my script. Would you mind starting from the top?"

She turned to face him fully, settling her gaze on him with a level stare. "Make no mistake, Detective. This is strictly a DEA operation. We're calling the shots. As my superiors have explained to your Lieutenant, the LAPD is being brought into this investigation merely to appease the local jurisdictional issues. Your presence is merely a token offering of cooperation."

"Now wait a minute, *Agent* Carmichael," Blake started irritably. Maybe if he wasn't close to burnout, he wouldn't have taken offense to her tone and haughty attitude. But he was tired, cranky and his fourteen glorious days in Hawaii had been preempted so he could baby-sit the DEA.

He took a step toward her. She didn't so much as widen her gaze in alarm. "I'm nobody's token anything," he said, reluctantly admiring her attempt to establish territorial boundaries early in the game. "You're in my sandbox now, honey. That means we play by my rules."

"The name is Special Agent Carmichael. You may call me Veronica, but I prefer Ronnie," she said, slipping a length of bobbed, sable hair behind her ear to reveal a pair of small gold, heart-shaped earrings. "In the future, I suggest you select one as a form of address as opposed to honey, sweetheart, doll or babe. If remembering my name is too difficult for you, then might I suggest you simply refer to me as Special Agent in Charge. It'd be a shame to have your sterling record besmirched with a sexual harassment complaint."

Blake glared at the sexy half-pint agent and counted to ten. Then kept going until he hit thirty-five. He'd never been prone to losing his temper. His skill for sweet-talking the toughest suspects into giving him the goods was legendary in the department. He'd always had a way with women, and the fact that the Southern belle in a badge seemed immune to his equally legendary charm, chafed. Nothing would have given him more satisfaction than to tell the department brass what they could do with their half-baked ideas about partnering him with an arrogant little DEA agent with more sass than smarts. The only thing that kept him from following through was the she-put-you-in-your-place smirk on Forbes's face. That and, despite being in need of a long vacation, he loved his job.

"I was just starting to fill Blake in on the case," Forbes said, motioning to the chairs in front of his desk.

Blake waited for Ronnie to sit before taking the remaining chair for himself. She gave him a bland look, then sat primly on the edge of the cracked vinyl. She placed the file beside her then smoothed her delicate, manicured hands over her skirt. Then, crossing her feet at the ankles and tucking them to the side in a perfect display of ladylike, finishing-school training, she turned that interesting gaze his way.

"Our preliminary investigation has revealed the primary activity to be in one of the island's most exclusive resorts," she said, folding her hands demurely in her lap. "For the past six weeks, we've had two agents in place working as employees of the resort."

Blake propped his foot over his knee and leaned back into the chair, still bristling over her haughty I'm-in-charge speech. "Why the need for another agent?" he asked. Avalon wasn't a large island, and in his experience with the DEA, they liked to do things their way, and without the assistance of other law enforcement agencies.

The phone on Forbes's desk rang and he picked it up, waving at them to continue.

"We know where the drugs are being manufactured and suspect the resort as a means of transportation," Ronnie said quietly, reaching for the folder. She pulled out a half-dozen glossy black-and-white photos and handed them to him. "We don't know who is involved. Unfortunately, our agents' positions in housekeeping and the resort bar haven't allowed them to develop any concrete evidence."

"And that's where I come in," Blake finished, examining the photographs. He didn't recognize any of the suspects' names or faces, but that didn't mean they didn't have records, something he planned to look into as soon as this meeting was called to an end. "I assume we'll be going in to obtain that evidence," he said, handing her the photographs.

Her smile was brief, causing that adorable dimple to wink at him again. "Exactly. Agents Anderson and McCall are working full shifts as employees so their time has been limited. Unfortunately, this particular resort plays to high-profile types and, as I mentioned, is *very* exclusive. They operate under a strict policy that doesn't allow employees to frequent the resort during non-work hours. Because of that, Anderson's and McCall's activities have been severely disabled."

"What makes you think we'll have any better luck?" he asked her.

Forbes hung up the phone and smiled pleasantly at Ronnie. "If you'll excuse me, Special Agent Carmichael, I have a meeting upstairs to attend."

Blake frowned. None of the detectives in his squad would ever call the lieutenant a touchy-feely kind of guy, and the kind, grandfatherly smile he cast in the pint-sized agent's direction struck Blake as almost comical. "Feel free to use my office for as long you like."

Ronnie slipped the photographs back into the file and flashed Forbes a charming grin. "Thank you, Lieutenant."

After crossing the room and opening the door, Forbes turned his attention to Blake. "Be prepared to depart for the island tomorrow morning," he said, using that commanding "I'm the boss" voice Blake was used to hearing. "Carmichael will fill you in on the rest."

The door closed and they were alone. Ronnie cleared her throat, making Blake wonder if she was more nervous than she appeared. Not that her demeanor would so much as hint at anything but ladylike calm, he thought. A more erotic image tripped through his mind, one that would have Ronnie Carmichael's cultured Southern charm slipping...right into his arms.

"The agency needs someone inside and allowed free rein of the island," she said, dragging his thoughts out of the bedroom and back to their conversation. "Our primary objective is to determine how the drugs are being moved through the island, as well as ascertain the key players."

"I understand DEA wanting to avoid jurisdiction problems, but you've already got two agents on-site hampered by resort policy. What makes you think we'll have any more luck?"

She lowered her gaze, her dark sable lashes sweeping downward. "Because we'll be going in undercover," she said, without looking at him. "Only not as employees."

The knot of tension returned and tightened, and he rubbed the back of his neck to help ease it. "But why me?" he asked, his voice filled with caution.

She smoothed her skirt again. "Your lieutenant explained you were the only officer he could spare...that fit the profile."

Blake frowned again. That twisting in his gut made a return visit, too, causing a riot among his insides. "Profile?" he asked, slowly lowering his hand. "What profile?"

Ronnie sighed and looked at him, her turquoise gaze intense. "I've read your file, Detective. Your experience in this area is well documented, and while there were other detectives with more experience, you are available and you fit the profile."

His frown deepened. "What profile?" he demanded a second time.

"You're thirty-one, right?"

"So? What does age have to do with an interdepartmental investigation?"

She tilted her head to the side, and regarded him skeptically. "Your lieutenant didn't tell you, did he?"

The churning increased, igniting a ball of fire in his gut that had him reaching into his pocket for the roll of Tums he'd starting carrying two weeks ago. "Tell me what?"

She pulled in a deep breath and let it out slow. "Detective, the resort under surveillance is Seaport Manor."

He shrugged and reached into his pocket. The name meant nothing to him.

She caught her bottom lip between her teeth. Her hesitation had his suspicion mounting. "Seaport Manor is a honeymoon retreat."

His hand slipped over the roll of antacids. "I'm still not following you," he said, refusing to jump to the wrong conclusion.

"We're going undercover, Detective. Tomorrow morning we board the Island Express, a water taxi which will take us to the quaint island resort and deliver us directly to the private dock of Seaport Manor, where we have two weeks to gather as much evidence as possible. We are registered under the name St. Claire, one of Savannah, Georgia's oldest and most prominent families."

His hand tightened over the roll of Tums. *"We are registered?"*

"That's right, Detective," she said with a brisk nod. "Blake and Veronica St. Claire will be spending the next two weeks at Seaport Manor as newlyweds." She flashed him a saucy grin, and a victorious light brightened her turquoise eyes. "Welcome to Operation Honeymoon. *Babe.*"

2

RONNIE FLASHED the too-polished and too-gorgeous-to-be-real detective a grin filled with satisfaction as his arrogance faded. Her own grin dimmed when his raven-black eyebrows collided over narrowed, pale gray eyes.

"Find yourself another cop to play house," he said, angrily pushing out of the chair. "I'm not interested."

Her smile disappeared completely. There *was* no other cop, and she had her assignment. Because of jurisdiction, she'd been forced to partner herself with the LAPD, rather than one of her own, for which she was secretly grateful. The last thing she wanted was to play loving wife to the very men who'd made her life a living hell the past three years. A fact that confirmed she should've followed her own dreams rather than attempted to fulfill a prophecy she'd never asked for, nor wanted.

She shifted in the chair as he reached for the door. "I'm afraid you have no choice," she said, grateful when the firm tone she tried managed to stop him from leaving. "While your department has been more than cooperative, you know as well as I do that deep budget cuts have left your division operating with the bare minimum. You're the only officer available. And I've been guaranteed—"

He spun to face her, his frustration-filled gaze connecting with hers. "I really don't give a damn what you've been guaranteed."

"Look, I'm sorry you're not happy about the assignment, but there isn't any other way." She didn't like him glowering down at her, so she stood and rested her backside against the desk. If he'd been standing in front of her, he'd still tower over her by a good ten inches, but at least she'd equaled the playing field...somewhat. "With employees being banned from Seaport Manor during their off-hours, we need undercover operatives on the inside that have the freedom to come and go as they please. And it *is* a honeymoon resort. If we went in as singles, we'd be suspect from the moment we stepped off the launch."

He let out a long breath filled with impatience. "You really think people are going to believe *we're* newlyweds?"

She gave him a brief smile, in hopes of placating him since they hadn't exactly started out on the best of terms. "From what I've read about you, Detective, you're very good at what you do. I'm sure you'll provide a convincing performance."

Something in his gaze shifted, sending a ripple of alarm skirting down her spine. His soft gray eyes filled with purpose as he crossed the cramped office, closing the distance between them. With every ounce of willpower in her arsenal, she held her ground instead of darting behind the desk like the little warning voice in her head was shouting for her to do.

He stopped mere inches away, invading her personal space, and close enough for her to breathe in the alluring scent of cologne and man. She cursed her rotten luck. Why couldn't they have found her a more middle-aged, less virile cop to play one half of the happy couple for the next week or two? Living in close quarters, in a ridiculously expensive and lavish honeymoon suite no less, with a man she found dangerously attractive held little appeal.

Or maybe too much appeal, her conscience taunted.

Definitely way too appealing, she thought. Since she knew the type so well, she could protect herself. Couldn't she? Forewarned was supposed to mean forearmed, not an invitation to lose control. Considering she'd once fallen victim to a guy with all the right words, all the right moves and all the wrong answers she'd been too blind to see, she'd just have to be extremely careful not to lose her head. She could never, for one second, forget Blake was merely a means to an end that would finally give her the chance to follow her own dreams for a change.

Oh, yes, she knew Blake Hammond's type all right. Cocky swagger and confident, killer smile, the kind capable of reducing any living, breathing female to a tongue-tied idiot. Soft, sexy bedroom eyes, combined with a deep velvety smooth voice warm enough to melt the iciest resistance. Throw in a body, hard in all the right places, yielding in even better places, and he fit the type to perfection. She'd sworn to stay away from *that kind* of guy, no matter how irresistibly charming. One momentary lapse of common sense was more than enough to last her a lifetime, thank you very much.

She shook the thoughts from her mind and concentrated instead on the tiny lines of fatigue bracketing Blake's eyes. She struggled to ignore the way her pulse revved when his gaze dipped momentarily to her mouth.

She would *not* make the same mistake twice, no matter how much her hormones clamored for male attention. Just to prove it to herself, she pulled in a steady breath. Almost.

"You've already threatened me with sexual harassment," he said, his voice filled with a calm she suspected was tightly controlled. "How are we supposed to behave like newlyweds with a threat like that hanging over my head?"

His meaning wasn't lost on her. Newlyweds not only spoke in endearing terms to each other, they touched, caressed and kissed...long deep kisses. Toe-curling kisses. Kisses that generated heat and fire and spelled trouble.

He shifted closer still.

She pulled back.

He followed.

She caught his tangy scent and nearly sighed.

"Newlyweds are in love and they act like it, *Special Agent in Charge*," he said, his deep voice soft and gentle like the touches, caresses and kisses he'd implied.

"You gonna file a complaint every time I have to do this, even if it means keeping us alive?"

He lifted his hand and cupped the back of her neck in his warm palm. Her breath stilled. His fingers sifted through her hair and sent a series of delightful tingles running over her skin. Reflexively, she placed her hand against his chest to hold him at bay.

Oh, big mistake, she thought, curling her fingers into a fist against the heat burning her palm. Surrounded by a solid wall of masculinity, damn if her feminine senses didn't go haywire. He was as solid as he looked, and the thought of peeling his neatly pressed shirt away to expose all that dark, male skin shocked her clear to the toes of her sensible beige pumps.

She was supposed to be past this silly kind of juvenile behavior. Lust had nearly gotten her killed. Lust along with misplaced trust in an agent operating on the wrong side of the law, something she'd discovered after it was too late. Big deal if Internal Affairs had cleared her of any wrongdoing. Her service record might not have been damaged because of her stupidity, but that didn't mean her heart and mind hadn't been banged up more than a little.

"I have my orders, Detective," she said with false bravado, despite the awareness shimmering between them. She fought hard to forget about bared skin and touching that glorious male body for the next two weeks. The thought of telling her family she planned to quit the agency and follow her own dreams would be far simpler in comparison. No matter how silly anyone thought those dreams might be. "And so do you," she added.

"Do my orders include kissing my 'bride' in public?"

She sucked in a sharp breath as the image of Blake's mouth pressing evocatively against hers flashed through her mind. "I'll do whatever is necessary to make this bust, Detective. If it means a kiss or two with my temporary partner to maintain our cover, then I will do my job."

He grinned, his devilishly handsome mouth filled with enough promise that her knees went weak in spite of her firm reminders. A mouth she'd be tasting soon enough considering their assignment.

"What about touching?" he asked, his voice low, like a whispered endearment.

"If I have to suffer through a few touches to keep us alive, then I'll do it. It's all part of the job."

"Suffer?" A sexy little smile tipped his mouth as he released his gentle hold. "I can't say a woman's ever told me she's *suffered* from my touch."

Ronnie seriously doubted the experience would be a painful one, and that was part of her problem. From the crazy way her heart was pounding, she had no trouble imagining all sorts of sensual delights his touch could bring. "There's a first time for everything," she countered, hoping to convince him, or maybe herself, she was immune to his devastating charm.

He stepped back and gave her some much-needed breathing room that did little to still the rapid cadence of her heart. Trading barbs with Blake Hammond definitely qualified as stimulating. Too bad other types of stimulation sounded equally intriguing.

He rolled his shoulders, then rubbed the back of his neck again. Ah, stress. Now there was something she could easily understand.

"I'm going home, Carmichael," he said. "I haven't slept in nearly thirty-six hours, and I'm beat. You're right. I don't have a choice, but before we go anywhere, there's one thing I want to make crystal clear."

She braced her hands behind her on the desk, hoping she looked more calm, assured and a whole lot more collected than she was feeling. "Which is?" she asked, arching her brow.

"I'll play, but we're playing my way. You can take it or leave it."

"You don't know anything about the case."

He shrugged and walked to the door. "That's why you're going to brief me. Tonight."

"Tonight? But—" She needed time to regain control. Something only distance would provide since she was nearly panting after Blake and all that incredible sex appeal.

"Tonight," he said, his tone as uncompromising as the flinty steel filling his eyes. "Be at my place by seven. It's in the file. I'll even spring for dinner."

She weighed her options, and couldn't find a single *professional* argument. He'd have to be brought up to speed, and she'd rather have him rested and attentive. Personally, the idea of being alone with him terrified her.

"Fine, Detective," she reluctantly agreed. "I'll see you at seven."

He gave her one last look, shook his head, then left her alone in the small office. She watched him through the open miniblinds as he stopped to say something to one of the other detectives before leaving.

Slowly, she moved to the chair and sat, willing her legs to stop trembling, wondering how she was ever going to survive a week, maybe two, pretending to be filled with lust for the sexiest man she'd ever met. Especially when the lines between pretense and reality had already begun to merge.

BLAKE TAPPED THE RAZOR on the side of the sink, silently cursing fate, and his lieutenant. The much-needed sleep did little to improve his mood, but considering his long-awaited and much anticipated vacation had been preempted, he figured he was entitled to a little crabbiness.

"Newlyweds," he muttered, scraping the razor along his cheek. He was no stranger to undercover operations. He'd been a detective long enough to have dealt with his fair share of assignments, good and bad, but none had ever evoked erotic images strong enough to haunt his dreams. Dreams casting a sassy, diminutive DEA agent with eyes the color of the sea, hair softer than down and skin as smooth and sleek as Egyptian cotton in the starring role.

Under normal circumstances, he'd never consider spending fourteen days in a romantic setting with a sexy, intriguing woman a hardship. Spending those days alone with a Southern belle with a badge and an attitude hardly qualified as an erotic fantasy. Agent Carmichael was a sexual harassment allegation waiting to happen, especially since he'd come dangerously close to kissing her this morning. Thank heaven his common sense had overruled his baser intentions.

Women and the badge weren't compatible. His parents' divorce when he was ten confirmed it. He had his own experience to quantify that knowledge, as well, not to mention more than half the cops on the force were either divorced or close to it. The divorce rate among the detective squad was even higher. Only a very special woman could handle being married to a cop. Not many understood the long hours, or how a disappearing act for days at a time when an undercover assignment came along was all part of the motto, To Protect and Serve. It took a strong woman to be able to deal with the reality that every time she kissed her badge-carrying husband goodbye in the morning, it could very well be the last time she ever saw him alive. In his experience, women like that were far and few between, one of the reasons why, at thirty-one, he'd never married. There'd been a close call once, but that was a lifetime ago.

He shoved those unpleasant thoughts aside as the doorbell rang. Rinsing away the remnants of shaving cream, he buried his face in a fluffy towel before heading to the front door of his beachfront condo.

He'd hoped his reaction when he'd first seen Ronnie Carmichael this morning had been a result of lack of sleep and extreme frustration. Those hopes crumbled when he swung open the door and his heart began to pound again.

She looked ready for a day of relaxing under the warmth of the southern California sun, even if she did have a briefcase in her hands. Her silky hair was pulled back into a short ponytail, a few stray strands teasing the curve of her jaw. Khaki walking shorts showed off her lightly tanned legs, and a teal cotton top with a scoop neck hugged her full breasts and emphasized her curves.

"Either you're independently wealthy or on the take," she said with a gentle smile, breezing past him. He caught the intoxicating scent of her floral perfume and breathed in, imagining the pulse points where she'd dabbed the fragrance.

He frowned and closed the door. "That's a hell of a greeting."

"You've got a nice place," she said, a bare hint of a smile flirting around the edges of her very kissable mouth. "I didn't know LAPD paid their detectives so well."

"They don't," he said, ushering her into the sunken living room overlooking the Pacific. "My mother's family has money and I bought this place a couple of years ago when I came into a trust. Not that it's any of your business."

She set her briefcase beside the glass-topped cocktail table and shrugged. "It's not, but I'd rather not be involved with a cop on the take."

"You have a really low opinion of cops for someone who wears a badge." He understood more than she believed, having his own experience with a good cop turning bad.

She slipped her slender hands into the side pockets of her walking shorts and turned her gaze to the picture window. Waves crashed on the sandy beach against a backdrop of red setting sun and dusky sky, perfect accompaniments for romance. Too bad Agent Carmichael was all business.

"I've seen a lot in the last few years," she said quietly.

"Suspicion or experience." Unfortunately, a cop turned bad wasn't as uncommon as he'd once believed. A recent experience with one of their own walking on the wrong side of the law still left a foul taste in his mouth.

"Experience," she admitted, then turned her attention back to him. "Nice view."

"I thought we'd have dinner on the deck."

Her sable eyebrows pulled into a slight frown and suspicion filled her turquoise gaze. "We're eating here?"

A note of panic filled her voice and he suppressed a smile. He'd suspected her interest this morning, but he'd written it off as his imagination since he'd been dead tired and feeling a little punchy. Perhaps his imagination hadn't been working overtime after all. Could it be his temporary "bride" wasn't as immune to him as she wanted him to believe?

"Unless you'd rather go to a more public place...where we could be overheard."

She shook her head and sat on the edge of the plush sofa. "Here is fine."

He headed into the kitchenette. "Something to drink?"

"Maybe later."

"I was thinking iced tea. We are working."

"Oh," she said, a slight blush covering her cheeks. "That'd be nice. Thank you."

She pulled the briefcase onto the sofa beside her and snapped the latch. By the time he returned to the living room with their drinks, she had a series of photographs spread over the cocktail table.

He handed her the iced tea and sat next to her on the sofa. She stiffened, then pulled in a long, deep breath. A dead giveaway of her nervousness. No way was anyone going to believe they were newlyweds. Not with her telling actions every time he came within two feet of her.

He leaned forward and scanned the photos. "Where are you from, Carmichael?" he asked, attempting to set her at ease.

She sat primly on the edge of the sofa, her knees pressed together, the iced tea gripped in her slender hands, a perfectly manicured nail tapping rhythmically on the glass. He had difficulty imagining those hands drawing, let alone using a weapon, even if it meant keeping them alive.

"I grew up in Savannah, but I live in New York," she said, "when I'm home. St. Claire is my mother's maiden name, by the way."

He set his glass on the table and used his neatly

pressed jeans to swipe the condensation from his hands. "Tell me something."

She kept her gaze riveted on the photos. "What do you want to know?"

"You don't fit. Not DEA."

She let out a puff of air. "It's a long story," she said, her voice filled with caution that heightened his curiosity.

She looked over at him and their gazes connected. "We've got all night," he said quietly, unable to quash the erotic images filtering through his mind *that* statement evoked.

"Three generations of Carmichaels have been federal law enforcement officers, starting with my grandfather. Two of my uncles, four cousins and my father are all DEA. It was expected that I follow tradition."

Two things struck him. First, her sweet, lyrical voice, devoid of emotion, as if her words were recited by rote. Second, the coldness that had entered her turquoise eyes. Both intrigued him, and made him wary. While he wasn't exactly thrilled with his newest assignment, the last thing he needed was a partner filled with resentment.

He leaned toward her, and eased the glass from her hands. His fingers brushed hers and she flinched before folding her hands in her lap. "Sounds like a prophecy you didn't want to fulfill," he said.

She frowned. "I'm an agent, Detective, and a good—"

"Blake."

Curiosity entered her gaze and her frown deepened. "Excuse me?"

"You'd better get used to calling me Blake if we're going to be 'married' tomorrow. You wouldn't want to blow our cover, would you?"

"Don't worry, *Blake*," she said. The smile canting her mouth failed to lessen his concern. "I'm very good at what I do."

"I don't doubt you are," he said, and meant it. She'd come prepared to work, and that impressed him. "But this isn't Sunday school, Ronnie. UC's know and understand the danger."

"I've been an undercover operative before. I know how to handle myself in a dangerous situation."

"Good. Then you know as well as I do that drug runners can be extremely dangerous, especially if we're talking millions of dollars that'll be lost once they're popped. People tend to get a little deadly when you threaten that kind of income, legitimate or otherwise. You keep flinching when I touch you or tapping your glass every time I get near you, how convincing do you think we'll be?"

"I don't know what you're talking about."

"I've been watching you, Ronnie. I move a little closer, and you start tapping your glass." To prove his point, he shifted closer. Bracing his hand on the back of the sofa, he leaned into her and glanced down at her hands. They were still clasped in her lap, tight enough to turn her knuckles white. "You're a dead giveaway, Ronnie."

She pulled back, as if to escape his nearness. He wasn't about to let her go anywhere.

"I always tap my fingers," she said primly. "It helps me think."

He narrowed the distance between them. "Sure it does."

"You don't know me well enough to make those kind of judgments."

"My hand brushes yours, or I touch you," he said, settling his hand on her smooth-as-silk knee, "and you jump."

"I didn't expect you to touch me, that's all."

He noted the panic in her voice, but refused to stop pushing her. If he was going in, then he'd be damn sure his partner was up to the assignment. With his hand still on her leg, he brushed his thumb along the curve of her knee. He'd expected her skin to feel as soft as it looked, and wasn't disappointed.

She pressed herself against the back of the sofa. With his other hand, he trailed his fingers along the curve of her neck and she trembled. "Tomorrow we're newlyweds. That means we have to convince everyone we come in contact with that we're in love and that includes touching." He smoothed his hand over her leg. She trembled again, but not out of fear or nervousness. The quick flash in her eyes told him loud and clear that this time, awareness ranked high on the list.

"I—"

"And kissing," he said, his mouth inches from hers. Her sweet breath fanned his lips. Only a will as strong as iron kept him from tasting her. "Once we hit the island, anyone we come in contact with has to believe we're married."

"But—"

"And intimate," he added, his fingers pressing against her wildly beating pulse. "Our lives will depend on a convincing performance."

Her eyes narrowed. "I can be very convincing," she said, her accent more pronounced. Another revealing nuance to her intriguing personality.

"Then prove it," he challenged.

"Prove it? How?"

"Kiss me. Kiss me like you mean it, Ronnie."

3

"YOU'RE BEING RIDICULOUS." Ronnie pushed away from him and stood. Before she could follow her instincts and bolt across the room, his hand snaked out and snagged her wrist.

"I'm dead serious," he said, his soft gray eyes filled with something unidentifiable that had her heart beating faster. "You're no civilian, Ronnie. You know what can go wrong as well as I do. You want to end up in a body bag? Because that's exactly where we'll be if there's so much as a hint we're not legit."

She wished he'd stop smoothing his thumb along the tender underside of her wrist. Didn't he know that drove her crazy and made her skin quiver?

Gently, she tugged her hand, but his grip tightened. "I'm no rookie," she told him.

"Great. Then you know we have to be damned convincing."

"Of course I do," she said irritably when he stood. Why was he doing this? Did he know the thought of kissing him had occupied her mind for the better part of the day? Was he aware of just how much she'd thought about slipping her arms around his neck and dragging his mouth down to hers the second he'd uttered that husky "kiss me" demand?

She hoped not, firmly reminding herself again that his presence on this case was nothing more than a means to an end. That's all he ever could be to her, no matter how many times her heart rate accelerated or how much overtime her imagination put in whenever she thought about the next two weeks alone in a luxurious honeymoon resort with him. He was her temporary partner and held no more importance than a vital piece of equipment required to do the job. She would not, could not, get caught up in all that sex appeal.

More significantly, Blake Hammond was a cop. And after what she'd suffered because of her former partner, getting involved with any man in law enforcement was nothing short of emotional suicide. One dark-haired, silver-eyed detective with enough sexual magnetism to short circuit her central nervous system *had* to top her list of males in the danger zone. She refused to be that stupid again.

He slipped his free hand along the side of her neck and used his thumb to tilt her chin up so she had no choice but to look into the steely determination in his gaze. "Then kiss me," he said, his voice a rough rumble of sound. "Kiss me and convince me I'm the only man in the world you want kissing you."

Against her will, the rate of her pulse picked up speed and collided with the hammering of her heart. "In case you haven't noticed," she said around the wedge of unease clogging her throat, "we don't exactly have an audience."

Without a word, he dropped his hand and gently tugged her wrist so she'd follow him.

"Where are we going?" she demanded when they reached the front door of his condo. She had no idea what kind of game he was playing, but she wasn't about to go quietly.

He opened the door. "To find you an audience," he said, continuing outside.

She hurried down the short flight of concrete steps in an attempt to keep up with him. "This is crazy. *You're* crazy."

He stopped at the base of the stairs and looked into the darkening horizon. "There's nothing crazy about wanting to stay alive. This way."

With a hefty sigh, she kept pace with him as he gently pulled her down a pathway toward a series of wooden steps leading to the beach. With his hand still wrapped around her wrist, they crossed the sand toward a strip of palm trees silhouetted against the murky skyline.

She peered into the darkness and spotted her audience. An elderly couple walked hand in hand along the shore, their bulky basset hound waddling and baying at the incoming waves, then romping down the wet sand after the receding water. Farther down the shoreline, a group of teens sat grouped around a fire pit. The scent of burning wood mingled with the salty tang of sea air, accompanied by the rhythmic beat of rap music from a portable stereo system, carried toward them on the evening breeze.

Blake stopped once they reached the palms, and

backed her up until her spine grazed the rough bark. "Put your arms around me," he demanded gently.

"I think you're taking this a little too far," she said, but slipped her arms around his neck just the same. While she didn't care much for his high-handed attitude, she'd been an agent too long not to understand the validity of the point he was trying to make. Their very lives depended on whether or not everyone they came in contact with believed they were the happy couple. How could they possibly hope to convince anyone if she continually avoided his touch? She'd just have to be strong and remember it was all make-believe. An assignment. More importantly, if they did their jobs well enough, it'd also be her last.

He settled his hands on her hips, his fingers pressing against her backside. "Like you mean it, Ronnie."

He wanted a convincing performance, then she'd give him one, she thought mutinously.

This was her duty, he was merely along for the ride, and if she didn't establish herself as the head of this little undercover operation, she'd be playing second string to the sexy, arrogant detective for the remainder of the assignment. And that was something she refused to allow to happen to her again. She'd been acting like a good little girl for too many years, and what had it gotten her?

Nowhere that she wanted to be again.

She toyed with the silky hair at the nape of his neck and looked into his eyes. "Just don't expect a declaration of love, Detective," she said in what she hoped was a husky voice.

"Blake," he said, dipping his head to nuzzle her neck.

She sucked in a sharp breath when his warm lips skirted along her jaw to her throat. She tipped her head back, not because what he was doing to her felt wonderfully delicious, but to provide a convincing performance.

Uh-huh. Sure, her pesky conscience taunted.

"Say it." His voice was low, deep and dancing over her nerve endings, adding to the delicious sensations his lips were already stirring.

His hands roamed from her hips and up her sides. His thumbs rested just below the underside of her breasts and she closed her eyes, an action that did nothing to quell the slow heat winding through the pit of her stomach, or the way her breasts suddenly swelled against the smooth satin of her bra.

He nipped at the sensitive spot just below her ear and she couldn't have formed a coherent sentence, let alone a hollow protest, if her life depended on it.

"Say it, Ronnie."

Her fingers flexed and tangled in his raven black hair. "Say what?" she managed in a breathy whisper, turning her head to the side when his mouth trailed a line of heat down to her collarbone. Between his mouth and that musky man scent mingled with the sting of sea air, she couldn't think straight.

"Blake. Say my name, Ronnie," he demanded again, while pressing biting little kisses up her throat and along her jaw. "Say it."

His mouth hovered over hers, his breath fanning

her lips more intoxicating than she'd ever dreamed possible. Good heavens, she *wanted* him to kiss her.

She opened her eyes and looked at him. Feminine pride rose within her at the desire flaring in his gaze. "Is it really necessary?"

"It is if you want to stay alive. My name has to be second nature to you."

She swallowed, knowing exactly why she was hesitating. Her mind might acknowledge it was only make-believe, but her body already had other ideas. Dangerous ideas. She knew he was absolutely right with every instinct she'd acquired since her first day on the job. Yet, somehow, speaking his name with his hands spanning her rib cage and his thumbs tracing lazy patterns beneath her breasts made saying his name far too intimate to be anything but real.

"Blake," she whispered, then gave in to the desire by pressing her fingers against the back of his neck, urging his mouth over hers.

His lips moved in an erotic dance of seduction that sent tingles of sensation shooting to her toes. Heat curled in her belly and spread outward as his tongue swept over hers, tormenting her with lazy sweeps until she trembled in his arms. He tasted sweet, like the sugar in the tea she'd drunk earlier. He tasted hard, like a pillar of strength, immovable and sturdy. He tasted hot, like mind-blowing, sweat-slicked bodies and tangled-sheets sex.

His hand slid from her rib cage and chased down her back to settle on her bottom. A moan bubbled in her throat and she molded her body to his, reveling in the feel of crisp denim against her bare legs, of the feel of his wide, firm chest against her sensitive breasts. Desire thrummed through her, and thoughts of regaining the upper hand fled in favor of the soulful, silky glide of his tongue exploring her mouth. He'd reawakened the lustful beast inside her, hot and primitive, guided by the natural, most basic need to mate. A need that shook and rattled her practiced composure.

One hand roamed her back and held her close, while the other smoothed along her rib cage and upward, this time cupping her breast in his large, warm hand. The music faded and her desire climbed when his thumb traced the pebble hardness rasping enticingly against her bra. The waves crashing on the shore dimmed and fierce need swelled, tangling her in a seductive web.

She'd experienced need. She knew firsthand desire could be a powerful emotion and more addicting than the drugs she worked to keep off the streets. She hadn't expected to be swamped with both by such a breath-stealing kiss that made her insides melt and her senses spin.

She slid her hands from his neck, over his wide shoulders and down the smooth cotton polo shirt to his firm, thick biceps, exploring the rough, male texture of his skin. She never wanted the kiss to end.

She pulled back anyway, silently cursing not only the instant loss of heat, but the fact that she desperately wanted nothing more than to slip back into his arms and finish what they'd started.

"Convincing enough for you...Blake?" she asked, surprised by the strength in her voice when the rest of her was trembling, as though she were a kitten facing down a Saint Bernard.

Slowly, his hands dropped to his sides. "Yeah," he muttered with a roughness in his tone. "Plenty convincing."

"Good." She lifted her chin a notch and hoped for a satisfied expression. Stepping around him, she headed toward the condo, feeling anything but pleased, but hot and achy instead...and wishing like the devil for an icy shower.

BLAKE WAS CONVINCED all right. Convinced he'd been lured into the lioness's den and had just been served up as the main course.

He followed Ronnie back to his place at a more sedate pace, needing time to rein in his runaway libido before he made another stupid mistake that had him sliding his hands over her lush curves and tasting the sweet perfection of her mouth. Instead of maintaining a keen awareness of their surroundings, he'd been consumed by her, something he couldn't allow to happen again. Mistakes of any kind were unacceptable, and often met with fatal results. Losing control definitely qualified as a drastic error, and it had nothing to do with the case and everything to do with the woman who'd just turned him inside out with need.

The kiss had been far from gentle, and filled with enough sizzling heat to scorch them both. He dreaded the thought of what could've happened if she hadn't ended the kiss. Making love to Ronnie was a temptation tough to resist, but was about as smart as stepping onto the ledge of a high-rise during an ice storm.

Not a smart move, he thought watching the provocative sway of her hips as she climbed the wooden stairs. For the second time in a short period, he'd lost control of a situation, and that bothered him. First, the suspect he'd been ready to pulverize, and now his reaction to Ronnie when she'd pressed her delectable body intimately against his.

He needed more than a vacation. He needed a reality check. A cold shower wouldn't hurt, either.

By the time he stepped inside the condo, he'd managed to regain a semblance of composure, until he saw her bend over to place something inside her briefcase. He let out a long, slow breath that did little to cool the resumed height of his temperature. Best to avoid the situation completely, he thought, and walked into the kitchen to place a call to the local deli for a couple of meatball sandwiches.

Thankfully, she kept her distance while he made himself scarce under the guise of slicing vegetables for a salad. They had a job to do, and he had no business blurring the lines because he couldn't keep his hands to himself. The department's non-fraternization rules were in place for a reason. Sex was one monster of a distraction and had no business on the job.

Ten minutes later his prime distraction sauntered into the kitchen with a smile pasted on her sexy mouth. A mouth he wanted to taste again and to hell with policy.

"Can I help?" she asked, her sweet accent breaking into his thoughts.

He considered telling her she could help by getting herself removed from the case and letting the LAPD handle it, or better yet, find herself another partner.

"No, thanks," he lied.

He didn't like the idea of Ronnie spending two weeks alone with another man any more than he welcomed the twisting in his gut the image evoked. He shoved the thought aside and attempted to concentrate on the mushrooms he'd been slicing, until she eased up beside him and braced her elbows on the counter. He glanced down as she reached into the glass bowl and filched a halved cherry tomato, his gaze drawn to the way her cotton top dipped, revealing the gentle slope of her breasts.

He let out another long rush of air that had little effect on his simmering lust.

She snagged another cherry tomato and smiled up at him. "I used to get my hand smacked for doing this as a kid," she admitted.

"Improper behavior for a Southern lady?" He pushed the bowl closer to her.

She laughed, a light sound that made him smile. "How ever did you guess?"

He finished with the mushrooms and started on the cucumber. "So is being a DEA agent."

She shrugged her slender shoulders. "Like I said, it's a family legacy."

He knew about legacies. He had his own he was determined not to fulfill, no matter how attracted he was to Ronnie. "So what do your prophetic instincts have to say about designer drugs being smuggled in and out of Catalina Island?" he asked, changing the subject...for now.

"We're supposed to gather evidence to determine who is involved, confirm the smugglers are using the resort, and if Seaport Manor is knowingly involved." She straightened and turned, resting her curvy bottom against the cabinet. Crossing her arms, she added, "From what I've studied so far, I'm seriously doubting there's any knowledge on the part of the resort."

"I called my lieutenant this afternoon," he said, despite his curiosity about Ronnie's past. "You know the resort's a joint venture, right?"

"Right," she said, looking suitably impressed that he'd done his homework. "But we've turned up nothing on any of the shareholders involved. They're so clean they squeak."

"Maybe all of them are legit," he said, rinsing a handful of radishes. "Or one or two of the so-called partners could be buried so deep, unless you knew what you were looking for, you'd never find it."

"Not a chance. The computers would have found something. Some link."

He flashed her a grin and shrugged, clearly not buying her explanation.

Her lips twitched as she pushed off the counter. "You're so doubting."

"Doubt has nothing to do with it."

She opened the refrigerator and pulled out the

pitcher of iced tea. "No," she said, refilling their glasses. "Then what does?"

"Experience." He dumped the last of the vegetables in the bowl and set the knife aside. "Do you know how many of these corporations are local? Not just California-based, but L.A.-based? All of them," he supplied without waiting for an answer.

"That's not unusual. Big resorts are owned by major corporations all around the world."

"Bingo."

She slipped the pitcher back into the fridge. "You lost me."

"The joint venture is a fake," he said turning to face her. "One, maybe two or three individuals tops are connected to Seaport, and he, or they, are deeply buried beneath a series of dummy corporations."

"That's impossible," she argued, shaking her head. "We've run each of those corporations through the computer systems and they all checked out. Believe me, if there were any links whatsoever, the system would have picked it up. The only connection is the joint-venture ownership of Seaport Manor. Period."

"You'll have to trust me on this one," he said as the doorbell rang. "I can feel it. We're looking for one person."

He left her alone in the kitchen and went to the door, returning a few seconds later with their meal.

"You're wrong," she said, taking the sandwiches from him.

He opened the cabinet for plates and place mats and laid them on the counter. "Avalon is filled with exclusive resorts. Over the last few years the place has turned into a corporate landowner's paradise. Every one of them are joint ventures or singularly owned by Fortune 500 types. All of them, except Seaport Manor, has the backing of big-name corporate dollars. What I don't like is the fact that Seaport is exclusively local."

She leaned against the counter and folded her arms. "Okay, I'll grant that it's not common, but you're forgetting a little thing called free enterprise. Our Constitution says it's okay for locally owned corporations to own a resort in the same town as the conglomerates on the New York Stock Exchange."

He set the meatball sandwiches on a serving tray with the salad bowl and dressings and led the way onto the deck. He should have his head examined for bringing them back into a romantic setting, but the June evening was warm, and taking his meals on the deck was a habit he enjoyed.

"This isn't about free enterprise, Ronnie. It's about a small phony band of investors, strictly *local* investors, using Seaport Manor as a front for a drug smuggling operation."

"We don't know that for certain. It took us a long time to get a strong enough line on what was happening on Catalina to even justify this operation." She leaned over the table to set out the place mats. "In everything I've read, there hasn't been one red flag on any of those corporations. Not so much as a single lawsuit pending, no SEC violations, not even a request for filing a late corporate tax return. Nothing."

He waited for her to sit before he joined her at the table. "That alone should be cause for suspicion."

"They're clean, Blake."

"They're too clean. It makes me cautious."

"I don't agree. Once the agency got wind of the smuggling, we sent out a few agents, and it still took them months to determine the drugs were even being filtered through the island. Like I said, we don't even know for certain the resort's involved."

"Then why did your operatives narrow it down to Seaport?" he asked, serving their meal.

"There's no other resort with its own private launch and water taxi," she said. She set a napkin in her lap, then poured a ladle of dressing over her salad. "The others have been watched closely, and turned up nothing. The problem is we haven't been able to get close enough to the private launch to set up an effective surveillance to know for certain."

He took the salad dressing from her, forcing his mind on their conversation and not the way her eyes shone in the early-evening moonlight, or how the light sea breeze ruffled her wispy bangs across her forehead. "What makes you think we'll have any more luck than your other operatives?"

She flashed him a grin filled with impudence. "Because one of their best honeymoon suites, bungalow number one, is less than a hundred feet from the launch, and has a perfect view of the surrounding beach. We'll be setting up a video camera so we can see exactly what comes in and what goes out, even when we're out of the room."

He braced his arms on the table. "Won't work," he said. "You're forgetting about housekeeping. That 'Do Not Disturb' sign won't be effective forever."

A becoming blush stained her cheeks and she cleared her throat. "One of our agents is working in housekeeping," she explained in a prim, finishing-school voice. "The other is a bartender."

"Not bad," he admitted with a grin. "What about days off?"

"We stow the equipment and break out the high-powered binoculars and 35 mm cameras."

"It's a start. Surveillance can tell us of any strange movement, but don't think it'll tell us who's involved."

"Of course it will. We'd have them on camera."

He leaned back in the deck chair and studied her momentarily. She was so dainty, so delicate. Too damn beautiful to be carrying a weapon and flashing around a badge. She also had tunnel vision, something he hoped to cure. "You surprise me, Carmichael."

She set her fork on the edge of her plate and let out a sigh before looking at him. "Somehow I don't think this is going to be a compliment."

He grinned at the caution in her voice. "For a DEA agent, you're thinking small."

She looked at him as if he couldn't think his way out of a paper bag with directions. "What exactly is that supposed to mean?"

"It just means I thought DEA didn't waste their precious collars on small-timers."

The narrowing of her eyes didn't detract one iota from the electrifying sparks of frustration flaring in her turquoise depths. "My assignment is to determine who and how the drugs are moving through the island. If we capture one of the people behind the smuggling, then the assignment is considered a success."

"Like I said, small time."

"I resent that."

"I'm sure you do," he said lazily. "But wouldn't a commendation for stopping whoever is behind the smuggling look a lot nicer in your service record? I know it would in mine."

"This isn't your case."

"Now that's where you're wrong, sugar. My sandbox, my rules. Remember? And my rules say we don't spend precious taxpayer dollars on grunts when we can bring down the key player behind the scenes, and send the whole operation into a crash and burn."

She tossed her napkin on the table. The sea breeze picked up, pulling more silky, sable strands free from their imprisoning band to caress her cheek. She angrily shoved them away. "First off," she said, a trace of genteel steel in her voice, "you don't know if there is a big player involved. And more importantly, this is a D—"

"DEA operation and you're in charge," he finished before biting into his sandwich. Fine. Let her think the winds of command were blowing in from her direction. He had a hunch. He always trusted his hunches.

"It's a good thing we're not really married," he said after a minute.

She folded her arms and tossed him another one of her irritated expressions. "Why?"

Damn, but she looked gorgeous when her feminine feathers were all ruffled. Her eyes sparkled, and the way she pursed her mouth had that dimple winking at him again. He wanted to kiss her. He decided to irritate her instead.

"Because sometimes, sugar, the man likes to be on top."

4

"ENJOY YOUR STAY at Seaport Manor, Mr. and Mrs. St. Claire." The desk clerk solemnly handed the leather-bound key holder to the bellman. "George will escort you to your bungalow."

Blake nodded his thanks and glanced down at Ronnie, noting the flash of what he could only term as strong trepidation in her brilliant eyes. He settled his hand on the small of her back to gently guide her after the bellman, who was already across the marble floor toward the rear of the lobby. Since they'd stepped off the water taxi, she'd been absolutely silent. While she might have suddenly lost her ability for speech, based on the perfectly straight line of her spine and the tension in her shoulders, she obviously hadn't lost her ability to stiffen whenever he touched her. He'd hoped after last night those telltale signs wouldn't continue to be a problem.

He'd been wrong.

On an assignment like this, he couldn't afford to be wrong. So what if his ego climbed a notch every time she flinched, stiffened or her intriguing gaze widened with wonder when he touched her. That wasn't the point. They had a job to do, and he swore before they took one step outside their bungalow, he'd make damned sure she had no misconceptions about her undercover role...as his *loving* bride.

They followed the bellman outside into a manufactured tropical world of romantic make-believe. He'd studied the additional photographs and video surveillance Ronnie had left with him last night, but even he had to admit the photos and video didn't do the place justice. Avalon hosted its own natural elegance and quaint simplicity, but the tropical additions by the resort designers made the reality of a drug smuggling operation almost surreal. Who would suspect something so devious in a location one step shy of paradise? No one, he thought cynically, which made Seaport Manor an almost perfect cover.

They continued to follow the bellman quietly along a winding brick path lined with thick foliage, from small palms and aloe vera to birds of paradise and just about anything that remotely resembled tropicana heaven. The path curved and branched out into four separate paths leading to various, secluded honeymoon bungalows, then split off again into separate, private courtyards complete with fountains and more imported tropical fauna and flora. None of which gave so much as a hint of anything illegal happening at the resort.

The bellman disappeared into the courtyard nearest the front of the resort that would provide them with not only a stunning view of the Pacific, but a fantastic view of the launches. Ronnie halted at the entrance marked by an arched, floral-covered entry into their own private patio. "It's breathtaking," she said, her voice a velvety soft whisper that stirred something deep inside him.

Against his will, his heart started thumping when he gazed down at her. Her brilliant eyes lingered on the romantic stage enhanced by the tall peaks and late-morning sunshine in the background. A cushioned outdoor love seat sat to one side of the private courtyard, nestled beneath the shade of leafy trees. From the rear of the bungalow stretched a latticed awning over the patio, providing shade for the table for two, set up for cozy, romantic dinners away from the other guests.

She closed her eyes and sighed slowly, causing him to momentarily suspend his disbelief about why they were really standing on the threshold of a honeymoon suite.

The bellman unlocked the doors and maneuvered the luggage cart into the room, leaving the white French doors open to the morning sea breeze wafting through the romantic village. Blake could manage nothing more than his full concentration on Ronnie and the way her eyes sparkled. A sweet smile curved her lips, a perfect rendition of unconscious seduction. God help him, he knew he was treading into dangerous waters, but the urge to kiss her, to taste her again, left him with a burning in his gut he found way too hard to ignore.

He moved in front of her, gently tipping her face up to his. "So are you," he said, wondering if he really meant for his voice to go all low and husky. Without bothering to wait for an answer to *that* burning question, he brushed his lips over hers in a feathery kiss. Male satisfaction reared up inside him when he felt her tremble.

Oh, yeah, this was going to be a very interesting assignment indeed.

He lifted his head. The smile curving her mouth remained, and was just as enticing as she'd tasted. He almost believed she'd enjoyed the light, lover's kiss as much as he had, except the fire lighting her eyes told another story that had nothing whatsoever to do with enticement or desire. She still looked sexier than any DEA agent he'd ever come in contact with, even if she was ticked at him.

"Was that really necessary?" she asked, her voice strained.

He smoothed his thumb over her bottom lip. For effect, he told himself. *Not* because her rose-tinted lips felt velvety soft beneath the pad of this thumb. "You never know who could be watching."

Her smile faded, and she narrowed her eyes before stepping around him. "I'd like to unpack now."

Wait just a minute, he thought. She'd trembled. Her lips had gone all soft and pliant. As far as kisses went, okay, so it wasn't his best effort, but, dammit, she'd still responded.

He caught up with her before she stepped inside their room. "Hold on there, *honey,*" he said, infusing a note of humor to hide the light battering to his ego. "Aren't you forgetting something?"

She gave him a look of narrow-eyed suspicion. When he dropped the carry-on bag slung over his shoulder on the low concrete landing, she took a hesitant step back.

"Blake, no," she whispered, guessing his intent.

He grinned. "Don't be shy now, honey," he said with a chuckle for the benefit of the bellman. "It's a honeymoon tradition."

Before she could utter a protest that might raise suspicion, he swung "his bride" up into his arms. Her soft curves pressed against him, sending a rush of activity south. When her arms slipped around his neck for support, her breasts brushed against his chest. Her nipples beaded and peaked beneath the silk of her pale yellow blouse and rubbed against his chest. His perfectly pressed Dockers suddenly felt a lot more snug than Levi Strauss intended.

"Put me down," she said, her Southern accent more pronounced now that she was so obviously nervous.

He ignored her demand and took the fatal step that would lead them right into another kiss. One that would be far from chaste considering their audience. "Now what kind of husband would I be if I didn't carry my bride over the threshold?"

"I can think of a few choice descriptions," she muttered dryly.

He forced a chuckle. "Don't be so independent, sugar. There are times when it's not an affront to your rights as a female to just let the man do what the man does best, especially when it comes to spoiling his wife."

"This isn't necessary," she whispered.

"Oh, but it is," he countered with meaning, then stepped fully into the room. "And so is this."

This had him slowly bringing their lips closer for a kiss. The deep, tongue-tangling kind that would be the equivalent of throwing hot oil into an already blazing inferno.

His name fell from her lips in a soft whisper. Whether it was out of protest or encouragement, he couldn't say. He figured it was the first, but allowed his ego to opt for the second.

His lips skimmed the softness of hers. She tensed in his arms, although surprisingly, she didn't clamp her lips firmly together. He took that as a good sign and pressed his advantage of the mediocre victory before she had a chance to retreat. His tongue slid over hers, tasting her deeply while quenching a thirst he hadn't realized he craved. Wanting to kiss her was one thing. *Needing* to kiss Ronnie made her as dangerous as their undercover assignment.

No matter how much the lady might protest, she still responded, albeit, tentatively. Almost shyly, Blake thought, something he found far too endearing and erotic considering she was his temporary partner. Her fingers played with the hair above his collar, then smoothed upward along the back of his head as if she didn't want the kiss to end any more than he did.

She pressed her body closer and he heard a soft little moan in the back of her throat. They were in deep trouble. There would be a lot more kissing, and definitely touching. If she continued responding to him this way, his legendary control would be finished for good.

The discreet clearing of the bellman's throat barely snagged his attention. With way too much reluctance, Blake ended the kiss. His breathing ragged, he slowly lowered her feet to the ground.

The bedazzled brightness of her eyes combined with unabashed desire made him uncomfortably hard. He knew she felt his arousal since she still had her arms locked around his neck, keeping their bodies molded perfectly together.

"Will there be anything else, Mr. St. Claire?" the bellman asked.

Blake cleared his throat and slowly peeled Ronnie's arms from around his neck. She looked away, no doubt embarrassed.

"Thank you, George," he said, digging into his pocket. "I think we can take it from here."

The bellman nodded his thanks as he took the tip Blake offered. "If there is anything you require, just call the front desk and ask for George," he said, then disappeared through the French doors, discreetly setting the carry-on Blake had dropped on the landing inside, before pulling the doors closed.

Ronnie disappeared into the bathroom without so much as an outraged protest. The sharp snap of the door followed.

Blake slowly lowered himself to the edge of the king-size bed and let out a rough sigh. About the only thing he'd be requiring was the return of his control, something he had a bad feeling he'd not be seeing anytime soon.

He concentrated on regulating his breathing, sucking much-needed oxygen into his lungs. He'd get through this. He'd been on worse assignments and could easily survive spending a week or two with an incredibly sexy woman and not touch her. Well, there'd be touching and a whole lot more kissing, he mused with a shake of his head. So long as he reserved those expected forms of intimacy between newlyweds strictly for public displays, he might just survive the assignment from hell.

Maybe.

RONNIE GRIPPED the rounded edge of the marble sink until her hands ached. Her breathing slowed and the rate of her heart steadied, saving a distress call to the nearest medical professionals. Physically, she felt a little more in control. Too bad she couldn't say the same for her emotions.

That easy, she thought, and she was all hot, achy and needy.

Again.

What was wrong with her? Kissing Blake Hammond was detrimental to the continued state of her mental health, and she knew it. Knew and even understood the dangers, yet she'd plastered herself against him and played a very willing participant in that kiss. Her toes had even curled. One sweep of his tongue and the man actually had her body primed and ready for more than just a kiss.

Again.

She looked at herself in the mirror and vaguely recognized the disheveled woman staring back at her. That woman's lips were slightly swollen and her eyes were still a little too dazed and confused to really belong to the Ronnie Carmichael she needed to be. That woman looked as though she enjoyed having her world tilted. As though she enjoyed being kissed senseless by a man that had more sex appeal than Heath Ledger and Hugh Jackman rolled into one spectacular specimen.

The Ronnie she needed to be wasn't supposed to respond to a tilted world or kisses hot enough to shake her psyche. The woman in the mirror was supposed to have been a stranger, not a familiar face she'd avoided for three years. Especially one that had come back to haunt her, reminding her of past mistakes, she thought with a frown. Even more frightening were those moments in Blake's arms when she'd wanted nothing more than to be that woman again. Wanted it more than her next breath.

She pushed herself away from the sink and backed up until she stood in the middle of the large bathroom. Closing her eyes, she drew in a few more deep, even breaths, which did zilch to restock her rapidly departing resolve. She needed to get her backside out there in the other room and face the man as if his toe-curling kisses hadn't had her toes curling. Not only was her emotional well-being at a stake, her professional integrity was in danger of being seriously compromised.

She dropped down to sit on the side of the bathtub large enough for four, and chewed on her thumbnail. Professional integrity be damned. She was just a big fat chicken, afraid of her own emotions and uncontrollable libido. Since when had she turned into a coward? Facing down criminals never spooked her. Never once had she shown a single shred of cowardice when it came to the job. One measly little detective with the hottest lips west of the Mississippi shouldn't have rattled her cage in the least.

She nearly moaned in agony. Blake had been doing nothing else but make her lose control since she walked into Lieutenant Forbes's office and had been rendered speechless the minute she looked into those soft gray eyes. She wrapped her arms around her middle and gave a pathetic little moan anyway.

The way she saw it, she had two options. Get out there and face him as if nothing happened, or camp out in the bathroom for the night.

Some options.

Well, she wasn't about to hide from him. This was *her* case, *her* investigation and, dammit, *she* was going to remember that. Controlling her lust and keeping it in check would be her top personal priority. Besides, she knew better, didn't she? She'd allowed her emotions to rule her once before and was still suffering from the aftershocks. Showing Blake she wasn't affected by him would carry a lot more weight if she wasn't sitting on the edge of an Olympic-size bathtub hiding out like a shy virgin on her wedding night.

She stood and squared her shoulders. "Focus," she

whispered quietly. "Focus on the job and nothing else. Be the agent in charge. You are in command of this assignment."

She nodded, liking the sound of that. "This is a DEA operation," she said, her voice a little stronger. "It's my responsibility. Now get out there and stop lusting after your partner."

A light knock sounded on the door. "Ronnie? You okay in there?"

Startled, she nearly squealed, but clamped her hand over her mouth before it escaped. She looked quickly around the elegant bathroom. If she didn't do something, he'd know she'd been hiding. No one could accuse Detective Hammond of being all beauty and no brains.

She darted across the plush royal-blue carpet, and flushed the gold-plated handle of the toilet. So much for her grand gesture of a take-charge entrance.

"I'll be right out." She made a huge production out of washing her perfectly clean hands, and breathed a grateful sigh of relief when she heard him move away from the door.

With no other believable distractions available, she had no choice but to face him. Schooling her expression into what she hoped was impassive boredom, she swung the door open and left her marble-and-gold sanctuary, determined to show Blake exactly who was the boss in this little undercover operation.

At least, she meant to until she stepped into the elegant bedroom with its rich furnishings and soft, romantic Victorian accents and found her way-too-distracting partner lounging on the very large bed. Blake looked ready, willing and more than able for just about anything her lustful conscience might suggest to pass the time. Suddenly, she was full of all sorts of interesting ideas, none of which had a single thing to do with the reason they were spending two weeks at Seaport Manor.

With his elbow propped on the mattress for support, Blake lay on his side, casually flipping through a ringed binder. His hair was slightly mussed, adding to his already oozing sex appeal. Damn him. Why did he have to be so gorgeous, so...*male?* Who had she ticked off, she wondered. Someone big, she guessed. And her punishment was to be saddled with a partner who turned her insides to partially melted Jell-O.

"Have you seen this?" he asked, spinning the binder around so she could see the bright, colorful brochure. "There's actually a lot to see and do here."

She opened her suitcase and plucked her casual cotton tops and shorts from inside. "You're not here to sightsee, Detective. You're here so the DEA can solve *their* case," she said, liking the authoritative tone of her voice.

He let out a rough sigh. "Blake."

"Whatever."

"No. Not whatever. Not Detective. Blake."

She ignored him while she pulled a small bag containing her toiletries from the suitcase.

"B-L-A-K-E." He came off the bed and approached her.

She spun around and slipped her lotion from the

bag to set it atop the dresser. Next to his cologne. "I know how to spell your name," she said, keeping her back to him. Now why would setting her lotion next to his cologne cause her heart to start fluttering? Ridiculous.

"You could've fooled me."

Unable to move, she watched him in the mirror and braced herself for his touch. Apparently her reflexes had decided to desert her since her feet remained rooted to the carpet like Dante's demon frozen in eternity. "I remember your name." Was that her voice, all wispy and seductive sounding? What happened to authoritative? Must be that woman in the mirror hogging the stage looking for an encore.

He lifted one of those midnight eyebrows and gave her that look of his, filled with barely-there patience.

"Blake," she said to appease him. She could think of a few words that were more flattering. Like sexy. Devilishly handsome. And *would you kiss me again?*

He took hold of her left hand and held it lightly in his own. "I thought we had this ironed out last night."

Ronnie tried to tug her hand from the warmth of his while struggling to ignore the sparks shooting up her arm and settling with electrifying accuracy in the tips of her breasts. "We did."

He disregarded her silent demand for release and stared at her for two heartbeats.

Anticipation hummed. Her toes flexed.

A slow grin tugged his lips. "Maybe this will help you remember."

He shifted his hold and extended her ring finger.

She stared in utter fascination as he slipped a beautiful, sparkling diamond ring on her finger. "Tell me this isn't real."

"Oh, it's real enough," he said, slipping his hands into his pockets.

"Where did you get it?" she asked him, examining the ring more closely. An intricate lace pattern that almost covered the entire band was filled with diamonds. She estimated the weight of each stone to be at least an eighth of a karat. After fifteen of those sparkling little eye-catchers, she lost count.

"The agency will never approve an expenditure like this," she said, looking at Blake. Her tummy did a flip at the sexy smile curving his mouth. A mouth she couldn't seem to stop thinking about kissing. "This baby has to be worth ten thousand dollars or more."

He shrugged carelessly before sitting in one of the upholstered Queen Anne chairs nearest the window overlooking the Pacific. "I was able to call in a few favors. It's on loan."

"Do I want to know from where?"

His grin deepened and her heart flipped over completely. "Probably not," he said. "Besides, you need something classy and genuine to fit the part."

The ring drew her gaze again. She'd never seen anything quite so stunning in her life. Well, she'd better not get too attached. The ring was on loan, from only God knew where, and was just a part of their disguise. So what if she'd imagined the look in his eyes when he'd slipped it on her finger as one filled with promise. The only promise either one of them had made was to solve the case. Period. She was letting her imagination get the best of her.

Again.

Giving herself a firm mental shake, she went back to unpacking, conscious of Blake's eyes on her as she moved back and forth between the garment bag and the closet.

Just ignore him.

Fat chance of that happening.

She put her suitcase and garment bag in the closet next to his, then set the case with the video surveillance equipment on the bed. Her body still hummed with the effects of all that anticipation, but she forced herself to concentrate on making certain the surveillance camera was in working order. When all she had left to do was press the record button, she set the video camera aside and slipped the tripod from the case.

"That's not a good idea right now," he said, returning to the chair. He propped his foot over his knee.

"Oh, really? Then how do you propose we watch the area around the clock?" She snapped the legs of the tripod in place. "We've been sent in to do a job and part of that job is surveillance."

He drummed his fingers on the arm of the chair, watching her as she slid the camera onto the tripod. "I'm serious, Ronnie. I wouldn't do that right now if I were you."

"You're not me," she said, peering into the viewfinder and turning the lens slowly until the detailed tapestry pattern of the bedspread came into sharp focus.

A light knock on the French doors had her lifting her head to look at Blake questioningly.

"I told you it wasn't a good idea," he said with a chuckle, and rose to open the door. "Ah, come in, George."

Blake stood aside as the bellman pushed a white-linen-covered dinner cart into the room. "The champagne and whipped cream you ordered, sir."

Ronnie had to give the bellman credit for his discretion. Other than a barely perceptible twitch of his lips, she almost believed he didn't even notice the video camera aimed right at the bed.

"Will there be anything else, Mr. St. Claire?"

Blake grinned widely and slipped the bellman another tip. Looking directly at her with a wicked, heart-stopping grin, he said, "I think we have everything we need now. Don't we, sugar?"

5

"YOU CAN STOP smirking anytime now."

Blake couldn't help himself. His grin widened. "Anyone ever tell you how adorable you look when you blush?"

She rolled her eyes and looked away, ignoring his teasing as she'd been trying to do since George's untimely delivery. It might have been effective if her gaze hadn't been filled with laughter or he hadn't caught her trying to hide a smile. He still couldn't say what made him call room service and place an order for whipped cream and champagne. The argument that he'd only been joking around in hopes of getting his "bride" to loosen up carried a modicum of weight, but he suspected his subconscious had something more decadent in mind. An invitation to a little sensual exploration maybe?

He put that thought on hold and followed her toward the hotel's main building. He enjoyed the gentle sway of her hips more than he should as she led the way to the resort's Sunset Bar, and between the tables to the far edge of the patio.

The overcast sky blanketing the southland so typical for June had lifted, leaving Catalina Island bathed in warm, California afternoon sunshine. A light wind blew across the island, rustling palms with mild gusts, jangling wind chimes and fluttering the large umbrellas providing shade over the scattered tables.

Blake waited until Ronnie was seated before sinking into the patio chair opposite her. The breeze gently teased the soft strands of her rich, glossy hair. His fingers itched to touch the silky texture, to let the satiny strands sift through his fingers. If he let the fantasy continue to run wild, he could almost taste her sweet mouth and feel the warmth of her lips beneath his.

He'd been feeling that way since he'd picked her up at her hotel in L.A. this morning. It'd been all he'd thought about during the previous, long restless night...alone in his bed. The strange, urgent need to touch her was as distracting as the desire that burned hot in his gut whenever he thought about her, looked at her, touched her. Obviously he'd been too long without a woman, because there wasn't another single logical explanation for his off-the-charts testosterone levels.

Instead of following through on any number of the delicious thoughts, he lounged back in the padded chair and watched her from behind the black lenses of his sunglasses. She'd changed her clothes before they left their room and was exposing way too much skin for his peace of mind. He followed the column of her throat and how the thin straps showed off the curve of her lightly tanned shoulders. The scooped neckline of her bright-print tank top only hinted at the cleavage hidden behind the fabric, but he practically started drooling when the silky material clung to her full breasts as she adjusted the cushion behind her.

He had to stop acting like a sex-starved teenager and start behaving like an undercover operative. They had a job to do, dammit, and it didn't include him losing his focus inside erotic fantasies and wishful thinking.

Forcing his mind on business rather than the business of seduction, he surveyed their immediate surroundings. Glancing around the outdoor bar, he took stock of the resort's clientele. An educated guess and he'd say they consisted of more than just honeymooners. Granted, all of the guests were couples, but they varied in age and came from nearly every walk of life imaginable. In addition to the requisite honeymooners, the guests ranged from the obscenely rich to the average, hardworking couple who'd probably saved for years or borrowed against their whole life policies just to spend a romantic week at the exclusive resort for lovers, perhaps to celebrate a milestone anniversary.

Not a single guest sharing the tables scattered about looked the type to be smuggling drugs through the island, let alone through this exclusive resort. His instincts told him the most illegal thing this crowd might have done in their pasts was nothing more innocuous than a little fudging on their income tax returns.

A shapely waitress in a short, tropical-print sarong came to take their drink order. He ordered a Mai Tai for himself, then looked at Ronnie over the rim of his

sunglasses when she asked for nothing more dangerous than a glass of iced tea, plain.

"We are on duty," was all she said once the waitress
was out of earshot, her tone as stiff and unyielding as
the rigid line of her spine.

He was having a hell of a time figuring her out. This
hot and cold routine of hers was frustrating. Even
when she wasn't giving off "don't touch me" vibes,
he'd have to be blind, deaf and dumb not to notice the
attraction between them. She felt it, too, and he suspected her stiff and unyielding attitude had more to
do with the desire he'd seen in her eyes earlier than
with good posture.

He slipped his sunglasses back into place, stretched
his legs in front of him and folded his hands over his
stomach. "We're undercover," he said, keeping his
voice low. They were seated close to the edge of the
deck overlooking the ocean, and far enough away
from the few patrons not to be overheard. "A drink is
allowed, you know."

She shrugged her shoulders, but wouldn't look at
him. "I prefer not to have my senses dulled or im-
paired."

He blew out a stream of breath. Okay, so maybe she
had a point, but they'd only just arrived. They still
hadn't worked out a plan of action or even made dinner reservations for that matter. This was supposed to
have been his vacation, he deserved at least one Mai
Tai.

"Agent McCall should be arriving soon," she told
him suddenly, in that same quiet voice filled with a

sexy genteel steel he found way too enticing. "We're supposed to rendezvous at thirteen hundred."

Why was she so uptight about everything? Surely she still couldn't be ticked at him because of the bad timing with the bellman and that room service order. She looked so prim, in that finishing-school way of hers. It made him want to ruffle her a bit, shatter some of that primness.

Shatter hell, he silently admitted. He wanted nothing more than to blow it to smithereens and take them both on a mindless journey that started with deep, wet kisses and ended with them both sated and spent.

The next two weeks were going to be long. He shifted in his chair. Long, hell, more like an eternity.

"That's one o'clock," she added with a smile and a bad stage whisper when he remained silent.

He nearly ground his teeth, but gave her a tolerant look instead. The waitress returned with their order and he managed to smile his thanks. He pulled in another deep breath and let it out slow, wondering where his legendary control had wandered to this time. Waiting for him in Hawaii no doubt, where he was *supposed* to be taking in much-needed R and R.

"We should do some sightseeing," he told her as he plucked a paper umbrella from his drink.

"We're not here to take in the sights," she said primly. "We have a job to do."

He lazily twirled the little purple umbrella between his fingers. Lazy was the last thing he was feeling. Edgy. Aroused. "Exactly," he said, then reached for the tall thin glass and took a long drink of the fruity rum concoction. Yup, edgy and aroused, with only one forbidden end in sight.

"I don't see how you can expect..." She shook her head, and what could have been the beginning of a smile teased her lush mouth. "Never mind," she said with a wave of her hand. "I understand. Get out, play tourist and see if we can pick up any leads."

He reluctantly set his drink on the frosted glass topped table. "I always find it interesting the things a person can learn about a place when they least expect it."

"I get the point, Det...Blake. There's no need to belabor it."

"Just making sure we're on the same page, sugar."

The slight narrowing of her eyes was her only reaction to the endearment. He flashed her a grin. "Speaking of sugar, I thought all you Southern belle types put tons of the stuff in your tea."

"I don't see how my drinking habits are any of your concern." To emphasize her point, she lifted her glass and took a drink.

Another surge of unaccustomed frustration nipped at him. He snapped the paper umbrella in two and tossed it onto the table. Leaning forward, he pulled off his sunglasses and gave her a level stare. "As long as we're in this together, everything about you is my business. I don't know how you do things in the DEA, but out here there isn't much partners don't know about each other. What you know can keep you alive. What you don't can kill you."

She frowned. "I didn't—"

"Look, I don't want to be here any more than you obviously do," he snapped. "But you'd better take that chip off your shoulder and start playing the game. And believe me, sugar, I play to win. So if it means sticking my nose where you don't think it concerns me, then that's just too goddamn bad."

She let out a sigh and pushed a stray wisp of hair behind her ear. "You're absolutely right. I apologize."

"Not good enough."

"I don't know what you want from me. Do you want to know that I'm a little apprehensive?"

"I want the truth, Ronnie. If you think you've got something, even if it's a hunch, you share it with me, and I do the same. We have to work together. You might not like me, but that can't be relevant. Not if we both want to stay alive."

She frowned, just a delicate furrowing of her perfectly arched brows. "I never said I didn't like you."

"You could've fooled me. Or is the timid virgin routine part of your cover?"

Her brilliant turquoise eyes widened in surprise. She opened her mouth, snapped it shut, then opened it again to say something that never made it past her strawberry-tinted lips.

"Lighten up and loosen up," he told her, leaning back into the chair again. "It's the twenty-first century, Ronnie. Not the nineteenth."

She scooted her chair closer to the table, then folded her arms on the top. "I am not a timid virgin."

"Then stop acting like one or people are going to start to get suspicious."

Her sable brows pulled down into a frown. "Excuse me, but weren't you there? In our room? In front of the bellman? Or was I kissing someone else?"

"What's your point?"

"I hardly call being plastered all over you behaving like a shy, timid virgin."

"So you do admit you like kissing me." He'd sure like her plastered all over him. A lot.

"Yes," she said, then shook her head. "I mean no."

"Which is it, Ronnie?" He smiled suddenly. "Yes. Or no."

She sat back in the chair, the beginning of a real smile curving her mouth. One that reached her eyes this time. "It doesn't matter since we're here to do a job."

"I think it matters," he said before taking another long drink of his Mai Tai.

She laughed. "No. Your overblown *ego* thinks it matters." After a quick glance at her watch, she stood. "We'll have to continue this discussion later. It's time to meet with McCall."

He took one last swig of his drink before standing and signaling the waitress for the check. After he signed the receipt, he and Ronnie walked in silence along the cobblestone path toward the private lagoons.

Once past the bungalows, the path ended beneath a floral-covered entry leading into what initially appeared to be an outdoor corridor of sorts, covered with climbing vines. Upon closer inspection, Blake was surprised to find a solid cinder-block wall beneath the vine, broken only by a series of four separate heavy doors, which looked as if they belonged in a medieval castle. Using the room key as the receptionist instructed when they checked in, Ronnie opened the last door on the left and led the way into a private, man-made temperature-controlled lagoon beneath a glass-dome ceiling.

Water rushed over the side of a jutting lava-rock formation, spilling into a blue-green pool surrounded by more of the rock and lush tropical plants and flowers. Tucked neatly in the far corner of the enclosed area was a cabinet made of the same rough wood as the door where, Blake assumed, guests would find whatever they might need to make their use of the private lagoon more pleasurable and enjoyable.

"Wow," Ronnie said, her voice filled with awe. "This is...it's..."

"Romantic," he finished for her. His heart started ricocheting around his chest again when his gaze landed on a cushioned, outdoor chaise off to the left side of the private lagoon. Nestled beneath another rock formation, it was surrounded by long vines that provided a curtain of sorts, falling from an overhang for shade. "Yeah. I think that's the word I was looking for, all right." She headed across the sandy floor to the cabinet and opened the door. "Can you believe this place? They have just about anything you could want in here."

Following her, he peered over her shoulder when she crouched to open the small refrigerator. "Anything" consisted of thick fluffy towels, a lightweight blanket, lotions, controls for a stereo system and a minibar stocked with the usual items.

She closed the door to the minibar and he cleared his throat. "Wonder what they charge for these?" he asked, reaching around her to pluck a box of condoms from the shelf.

She turned a heavenly shade of pink. "Put those back!"

"Come on, Ronnie," he laughed. "We're both adults here."

She snagged the box from his hand and set it back inside the cabinet next to various bottles of lotion he bet a day of his precious vacation were edible. "Who won't be needing those, thank you very much."

The soft click of the door caught their attention. Ronnie slammed the cabinet door shut and danced away from the evidence of her snooping.

"McCall," Ronnie said in greeting, the smile fading from her lips. That trace of well-mannered steel reappeared in her voice, along with an iciness that made Blake curious.

The other agent closed the door behind him and flipped the lock for privacy before sauntering toward them. "Wouldn't want anyone to walk in on us," he said. "Those locks keep other guests out if the lagoons are in use."

Interesting, Blake thought, but quickly quashed the erotic musings playing on the fringes of his mind. He was here to work, he sternly reminded himself, not play out some desert island fantasy.

Instead, he leaned casually against the cabinet door

and studied McCall. He reminded Blake of one of those career lifeguards who spent their time working on their tans and being hit on by dozens of beach beauties. Blake wasn't sure what he expected to find, but a young pup who looked barely old enough to be out of high school, let alone a seasoned undercover operative, was not it.

McCall stopped a few feet away. Upon closer inspection, the agent didn't look quite as young as Blake first imagined. When McCall's blue eyes swept Ronnie, taking in the length of her tanned legs, the gentle curve of her hips beneath a pair of khaki-green walking shorts and the thin, silky material of her print tank top, Blake bristled, not liking the appreciative light that entered the guy's eyes.

"Looking good, Carmichael," McCall drawled. "Too bad I was already on site as a bartender. We could've had some fun playing house."

"Scott, this is Blake Hammond," she said, ignoring McCall's snide comment. "He's my partner for this assignment."

Blake shook the hand McCall extended, resorting to a juvenile, Neanderthal pissing contest by applying a little more pressure than usual. He didn't appreciate the way the other agent kept looking at Ronnie as if she was some prime morsel waiting to be devoured. And he sure as hell didn't like the corresponding twisting in his gut in response to McCall's comment.

Jealousy?

Hardly.

Maybe.

"Can I safely assume you've been brought up to speed?" McCall asked him. He reached into his shirt pocket and withdrew a pack of cigarettes, offering one to Blake.

"You can," Blake said. He didn't smoke as a rule, but took one anyway. Well, there were those occasions with the guys at Charley Walker's, a pub near the station house owned by a retired cop, when a cigarette and frosty mug of beer tasted damned good after a long day, even if the next day his throat did feel a little like he'd swallowed ground glass.

Ronnie stared at him as he lit the cigarette and took a deep drag. "I didn't know you smoked."

"I don't."

"Then why are you doing it now?" she demanded, her voice heavy with censure.

McCall chuckled. "Careful, Carmichael. You're starting to sound a lot like a wife."

She gave the other agent a barely tolerant look. "I wonder what *your* wife would have to say about that comment?"

"So what do you have?" Blake asked McCall, drawing the conversation back to the case and hopefully away from the tension between the two agents. Something was up, something he hadn't been made privy to, and it bothered him. What was it he'd said to Ronnie? What you don't know can kill you?

"There's some buzz going around this big shot's coming in again tonight. Guy owns a yacht, throws anchor and uses the private launch."

Blake shrugged carelessly, feeling a little more like

his old self. Cool. Calm. In control. Focusing on the job at hand rather than the woman making his body pound with need had a lot to do with it, he was sure. "That's not so unusual. Seaport's a high-dollar resort. It's supposed to attract that kind of clientele."

"Yeah, but the guy's been here a few times since I've been on-site. First couple of times, okay. Brought his big boat, stayed for a few days then came back ten days later for another visit. Could've been a stopover on a return trip. Except the same routine all over again, ten days later."

"And now he's back again," Ronnie said. "How long since he was last here?"

"Ten days," McCall said. "Like clockwork."

"Couldn't just be a coincidence?" she asked.

Blake shook his head while he finished the cigarette and tossed the remains into the foliage. "Too much of a pattern to be a coincidence." He looked at McCall. "I didn't see anything in the reports about this guy."

"It's a somewhat recent development," McCall said, then took a deep drag on his cigarette.

Blake nodded, but suspected otherwise. "What do you know about the guy?"

"I've had the agency run a sheet. Other than a few minor possession busts about ten years ago, the guy's been clean."

"Who is he?" Ronnie asked.

"Alister Clark," McCall answered her. "Served him a couple of times over in the Sunset Bar. From what I can tell, he's a hotshot around L.A. Name mean anything to you, Hammond?"

Every instinct in Blake sprung into full alert, shattering what he'd hoped was the return of his trademark stoicism. Oh, yeah. He knew Clark all right. The bastard might look clean on a rap sheet, but he was dirtier than a crooked politician and someone the vice squad had been unsuccessful in nailing for years because there was never any way to connect him with a crime. If anyone knew how to bury himself behind dozens of dummy corporations, it'd be Alister Clark. "I don't know. Maybe," he lied. "You said he's coming in tomorrow?"

"Uh-huh. I'll keep my ears open and let you know if I hear anything."

"I'll get word to my partner and have him check into Clark. See if he can come up with anything." Luke wouldn't be able to find anything more than what McCall had already unearthed, but it'd buy him some time to figure out what to do next.

Ronnie tucked her hands into the pockets of her shorts. She cast a surreptitious glance in Blake's direction. So much for his grand speech about sharing everything with your partner. He knew something about this Clark character and he was keeping it to himself. He had to be, based on the way his body tensed when Scott mentioned his name. For some reason, Blake was playing it low-key. She was determined to find out why just as soon as this meeting concluded.

McCall checked his watch. "I gotta report in to the bar and not get caught leaving here. You two newlyweds have fun."

"Let's meet tomorrow night. Unless something develops before then," Blake said.

McCall nodded. "Carmichael will know how to find me." His lips twisted into a half grin. "That is unless she forgets who the good guys are again."

She glared at Scott. "That's enough, McCall. I was cleared and you know it."

"Whatever, babe," he said, the condescending tone of his voice grating her nerves. "Everybody makes mistakes."

He turned and headed for the exit, not bothering to clarify whether he'd meant Internal Affairs made a mistake in clearing her, or something much more personal. Either way, she was positive casting doubt had been his intent. From the day she walked into the sacred halls of the DEA, she'd battled belittlement by her fellow agents. They resented her not only because she was a legacy, but because of her gender. It didn't matter that she'd received no special treatment just because she was a Carmichael. She was a woman, and she didn't belong in their ranks as far as her colleagues were concerned. Since the day she'd been sworn in, their narrow-minded attitudes had caused her nothing but grief. Couple that with her drastic error in judgment by letting her heart, or her hormones, influence her, and her life had been a living hell for three years running.

Two more weeks, she told herself. Two more weeks and she'd leave it all behind. She'd never wanted a career in law enforcement. In fact, her career goals were the polar opposite of the criminal justice system. The one time she'd dared to mention her own wants and needs, she'd received resistance. Better to go along and get along. Well, no more. She was more than ready to embark upon her own future with her own goals. At least once she and Blake managed to bust whoever was behind the drug trafficking.

Blake's warm hands landed on her shoulders as he turned her around to face him. A fierce light shone in his eyes, chasing away the warmth and teasing he'd shown her when they were snooping through the cabinet. "You want to tell me what the hell that was about?"

"An old argument you don't need to concern yourself with," she told him, attempting to shrug off his touch.

His fingers bit into her flesh. "I'm not buying it, Carmichael. What's going on?"

"It's old news."

"It don't care if it's last year's headline. No secrets, Carmichael. You either tell me what the hell that was all about, or the honeymoon is over. Today."

6

"I THINK THE QUESTION of the day is, what do you know about Alister Clark?"

Blake dropped his hands from her shoulders. He hadn't even realized he'd given himself away when McCall mentioned Clark's name. "What makes you think I know anything about him?"

"Oh, be serious, Blake," Ronnie said, folding her arms in front of her. "I was standing right next to you. When Scott mentioned his name, you were ready to burst."

He shrugged to buy time. To test his instincts? Or hers? Or was her question merely a diversion from his own demand? He didn't like to think so, but he wasn't going to take any chances. "Maybe I just didn't like the way the guy was looking at you," he said after a moment.

One of her sable brows rose and a half smile canted her mouth. "You'd never make it as a criminal, Blake. You're a horrible liar. You know something, now what is it?"

He let out a sigh and decided to play it straight with her. After what he'd told her about honesty between partners, he didn't have much choice without calling himself a hypocrite. "I've never personally had any contact with the guy so there's no risk of our cover being blown if that's your concern.''

"Partly," she admitted, her turquoise gaze intent as she waited for an explanation. "But you know of him."

He nodded. "Long before I ever moved into Vice, Clark used to run with a real ugly character, Devlin Shore, who's been tucked away in San Quentin for the last couple of years. Those minor drug possession charges McCall mentioned were courtesy of my former partner. There hasn't been much on Clark in recent years, only because the vice squad can never seem to finger the guy for anything. He's good at hiding."

"So why not say anything to Scott?" she asked. "And more importantly, were you even going to tell me?"

"If I'm right, the last thing we need is for McCall to alert the guy. And yes, I planned to tell you. I just didn't want to say anything until I had Luke do some checking." Not exactly the truth, but close enough to keep out of hypocrite status for the time being.

Something about her expression changed. Relief? he wondered. It made him nervous and cautious, and he didn't like feeling either because those kind of emotions dulled the gut instinct cops relied on to stay alive.

"Scott might be a jerk most of the time, but he's a good agent."

"I didn't say he wasn't, but I have a feeling he can be a little overzealous." At the slight nod of her head, he continued. "If Clark is involved, which my hunch says he is, then the last thing we want is for him to get suspicious and slip away. Like I said, this creep has a long history of hiding."

Ronnie felt a stab of guilt for diverting the conversation away from Blake's questions about her past, but she'd always been a private person. Never one to lay open her heart and share her innermost feelings, she certainly wasn't about to tell him about the biggest mistake of her career, or her life for that matter. Nor did her refusal to tell him stem from not wanting him to know she'd been weak, that she'd played right into her partner's hands because she'd been blinded by his good looks and smooth-talking ways.

In any case, she didn't care for the answer to *either* question any more than she appreciated the fact her future was still being affected by her past. Between her own mistakes and fulfilling a legacy she'd never wanted in the first place, she had days when she felt her past would haunt her the rest of her life. The sooner she got out of the DEA, the sooner she could reclaim her life. Fulfill her own dreams for once rather than those of another person.

When she remained silent, he said quietly, "Okay, Ronnie. You got your answer. Now I want mine."

"There's nothing to tell," she said quickly. Too quickly, she suspected, based on the slight lifting of his eyebrows. She moved around him and headed for the door. "We really should go. Someone might want to use this...place."

Blake beat her there and turned the bolt for privacy.

With his arms crossed over his chest and his feet braced apart, he looked down at her. Lord, he was a gorgeous specimen.

"As newlyweds," he said patiently, "we're just as entitled to the private areas as any other guests. So until you tell me what the hell McCall was talking about, we aren't going anywhere."

So much for her diversionary tactics. Why couldn't he be all beauty and no brains? Just her luck, she'd been partnered with a smart one with finely tuned instincts.

"Your silence is making me nervous," he said when she just kept staring at him. "Talk to me, Ronnie."

Conversation was highly overrated, especially when she'd much rather give in to those other, more sensual thoughts racing through her mind. The pale light filtered through the glass ceiling made his thick dark hair shine and his soft gray eyes look inviting. Her gaze dipped to his mouth.

It'd been such a long time since she'd felt pure lust, but the feeling was far from foreign. Since she'd met Blake she'd been experiencing a lot of strange sensations that had lain dormant for three years. Maybe she just needed to get laid. Guys did it all the time. Women got tense. Was it a crime to want to relieve some of that tension the old-fashioned way? What was so wrong with a woman wanting to have sex just for the sake of having sex?

For her, everything. No matter how much she told herself she could embark upon wild, uninhibited, and no doubt extremely satisfying sex with her temporary partner, experience had taught her a different lesson. There was no such thing as sex for her without her heart getting involved.

If she offered, he'd accept, too, which made the temptation even more dangerous. There was no denying the chemistry between them. A guy like him probably knew all about chemistry and how to use it to his advantage without letting his heart get involved. He no doubt had more than his fair share of women and knew how to walk away without a care in the world. Unfortunately for her, sex always went deeper, usually right into territory where the terrain was far too emotional on a path that led straight to a broken heart, or worse, as it did the last time.

Anything can happen, if you let it.

Well, she wouldn't let *it*.

"It's ancient history," she finally said. "And has nothing to do with the case."

"Maybe not, but I'm curious. Enlighten me."

"Why?"

"It matters."

"It shouldn't matter. We hardly know each other for one thing," she argued. At least he wasn't supposed to mean anything to her, other than her being his temporary partner on a temporary assignment.

"Professionally it matters, Ronnie," he said, still looking down at her with a hefty dose of determination shimmering in his gaze. "Considering my previous experience with a cop who forgot who the good guys were, can you blame me?"

She rolled her shoulders in a vain attempt to lessen the tension building in her neck and shoulders.

"Dammit, Ronnie. Say something? Your body language is screaming you're guilty as hell."

"Why do you care?" she snapped, feeling hemmed in and defensive. Dredging up the past made her feel that way. Facing the truth of her own actions, combined with the guilt she'd never been able to shake, didn't help, either.

He swore ripely. The tension was clearly making him just as edgy. "Look, if there's a problem, I'd rather know now than before it's too late. An innocent woman's life was put in jeopardy and a damn good cop was shot in the line of duty because one of our own turned sour. That's not a scenario I'd like to repeat."

"Neither would I," she said in a calmer tone. "It's not what you're thinking. I had an affair with my partner and it just turned out...to be a mistake." Not exactly the whole truth and nothing but the truth according to her, but it was as close to an admission as she was willing to give.

He watched her closely and she waited, hoping he'd accept her thinly veiled version of the truth. Finally, he relaxed and she nearly let go a huge sigh of relief.

"Most affairs in the workplace are a mistake," he said, his tone turning gentle. "There's a reason for all those no-fraternization policies."

"Yes, well, live and learn," she said, her voice sounding overly bright and slightly brittle as she stepped around him to reach for the door lock. "It's not a mistake I plan to repeat."

He turned and muttered something that sounded a lot like "too bad." She thought so, too, but pretended ignorance and opened the door.

"If Clark's coming in tonight, we have work to do," she told him, using her backside to hold open the heavy door. "You have a phone call to make and we need to come up with the best way to utilize the information from Scott."

He hesitated, and she held her breath, hoping he'd take the hint and accept her changing the subject on him, again. After what felt like an eternity, he motioned for her to leave the private lagoon. Suddenly, she was breathing a whole lot easier. Even if she suspected she hadn't completely convinced him that there was nothing more to her story than what she'd told him.

"I don't suggest using the phones around the resort," she said, keeping her voice low as they walked through the village back to their room. "Just a precaution."

"I hadn't planned on it," he told her.

She bit her lip, not quite sure how to proceed with her next request. Blake was a distraction, one she couldn't afford if she planned to leave the agency. In order to do that, she desperately needed to solve this case and get that hefty bonus promised to her. Combined with her savings and small investment portfolio, she'd have the start-up money for her own business. She had a trust fund from the St. Claire side of the family, but that money was tied up, and other than a quarterly stipend, the funds were out of her control.

By the time they reached their bungalow, she still hadn't figured out how to tell him about the sexual boundaries she set for the next two weeks. She followed him into the room and closed the door.

"Get whatever you need for sightseeing duty," he told her. "I'll call Luke from a pay phone."

She leaned against the French door with her hands pressed against the warmth of the glass. "Blake?"

"Hmm," he murmured, his mind obviously elsewhere as he opened the top drawer of the dresser. No doubt he was thinking about the case. If only she could be as single-minded. And that was exactly what she wanted to talk to him about.

"There's something else we need to discuss."

He closed the drawer and looked at her. "Sounds important."

She sighed. "It is. I don't think it's a good idea if we...well, you know."

He propped his elbow on the tall dresser. The look in his eyes could only be described as amused. "No, I don't know, but I suppose you're about to enlighten me."

She let out another huff. "Don't make this difficult."

"Make what difficult? You're not being especially explanatory."

"Do I have to spell it out for you?"

He shrugged carelessly as his grin widened. "Looks that way."

"Fine," she said, and pushed off the door. Refusing

to look at him, she walked across the room, past that big bed she'd have to share with him unless she planned to sleep on the floor, to the closet.

"Ronnie?"

"What?"

"You were going to spell it out for me."

She really hated the laughter in his voice. "We shouldn't touch. Or kiss. Unless it's absolutely necessary."

"Does it bother you?"

Well, yeah. As in *hot* and bothered.

She pulled a lightweight sweater from the closet before sliding the mirrored door closed. "We can't allow ourselves to become distracted," she said, slipping her arms into the sweater. "We do have a case to solve."

"I distract you?"

She rolled her eyes, hating that he was humoring her. "Yes, Blake, you do. We're supposed to be concentrating on the case. Especially now that we have a possible lead."

"I see," he said slowly. "What do you suggest? So I don't distract you, that is."

The man could not be that obtuse. She cleared her throat. "We should keep public displays of affection just that—public. There's really no need for us to touch or kiss when it isn't necessary to the case."

He nodded. "Only when it's necessary."

"Only when *absolutely* necessary," she added. "So we understand each other then?"

He chuckled. "Yeah, Ronnie. I understand you. Shall we leave now?"

For some reason, she didn't feel exactly confident that he fully understood her meaning, but she was willing to let the subject drop. She'd already done more than enough to inflate the man's oversized ego. So long as he was willing to do his part so they could concentrate completely on the case, then she'd be happy.

Frustrated, but happy.

A DAY OF SIGHTSEEING in the town of Avalon hadn't garnered them one iota of information with regard to Alister Clark, nor of any strange comings and goings on the island. As had been previously reported by the other agents on-site, Seaport Manor seemed to be the optimum location for smuggling drugs. It all came back to the private launch and the appearance of Clark's yacht every ten days. Not much to go on by any stretch of the imagination, but it was all they had so far.

Blake made one last adjustment to his tie before slipping into the charcoal-gray suit jacket. "You about ready?" he called. Ronnie had been in the bathroom dressing for the last hour and a half. If she didn't get the lead out they'd be late for their dinner reservations in the hotel's main dining room.

What was it with women and bathrooms? What was it with women, period? Especially his partner who'd somehow managed to get under his skin. Maybe it'd been the way she'd tried to tell him he distracted her that had kept his imagination revving, but

ever since her latest edict he'd been able to think of little else.

He glanced back at the bathroom door and considered barging in on her if it meant moving her along.
Before he could act, the door swung open, shocking
him into stunned silence.

Ronnie might be the first woman in too damn long
to stir not just his mind with erotic musings, but his
body, as well, but she was still his partner. She did
have a point about distractions, and looking at her
now, the full import of her earlier comments never
rang more true.

He really shouldn't be rendered speechless by the
sight of her dressed to kill, but his brain obviously decided it was in need of a little short circuiting. The little black number teased curves his hands itched to ex-
plore, evoking even more pesky musings of what
sensual delights awaited him beneath the silky-
looking material of her dress. There were no sleeves to
speak of, just a scrap of fabric that held the dress in
place off her lightly tanned shoulders, then dipped to
an enticing heart-shaped curve above the gentle slope
of her breasts.

Damn, but she was gorgeous. If he kept his promise,
other than a few touches for the sake of their cover,
Special Agent Ronnie Carmichael was off-limits.
Damn.

"I didn't know the classic little black dress was part
of the DEA's standard uniform," he said, after his
brain resumed functioning with a semblance of nor-
malcy.

She practically glided across the room to the dresser in her stocking feet, like an apparition too surreal to be anything but a dream. A very vivid, erotic dream.

"It's a necessity in this case," she said, stooping carefully to pull open the bottom drawer of the dresser.

His mouth went dry at the sight of all that skin exposed beneath sheer black nylons. "Nice necessity." The guys at the precinct could complain all they wanted about women partners. They obviously never had one as delightfully appealing as the petite DEA agent playing hell with his testosterone level.

She retrieved a red satin jewelry bag from the drawer and set it atop the dresser. Carefully untying the matching ribbon holding the bag closed, she laid it open and sifted through the sparkling contents. "Thank you," she said, a hint of laughter in her voice.

After slipping a pair of pearl earrings into her lobes, she tied up the bag again and returned it to the drawer.

He caught a glimpse of the lacy tops of her black nylons and his stomach clenched. Oh, man, was he ever in trouble. He couldn't stop thinking about what other lacy secrets were hidden beneath that dress.

Off-limits. Off-limits, he repeated silently. Uselessly.

He scrubbed his hand down his face. His semi-aroused state had grown to a full-blown hard-on. A romantic candlelight dinner followed by holding Ronnie in his arms for a few slow dances were bound to render him incapable of rational thought, or behavior for that matter.

Watching a woman slip into a pair of high-heeled black pumps shouldn't have been the sexiest sight he'd seen in ages. Breathing in the intoxicating scent filling the room as she dabbed a high-dollar perfume behind her ears and on the pulse points at her wrist shouldn't have been the most seductive act in the history of men and women. There was no point in denying both mundane, everyday actions were adding to his already near-crazed state. The only consolation to his reawakened libido was that the attraction was definitely mutual. Why else would she have called him a distraction?

She turned to face him, her gaze skimming over him. He easily imagined her hands doing the same, sliding over him slowly, exploring...the sharp ache in his groin stole his next breath.

"You're absolutely beautiful," he said with meaning.

She smiled, just a sweet curving of her luscious-looking mouth that had him wanting to taste her again. Bad. Real bad.

"I think we covered that already," she said quietly, "but thank you."

He sucked air into his deprived lungs. As much as he hated to admit it, she was right. Sex was a distraction. But Ronnie in that dress presented one hell of a temptation he was finding hard to resist.

Where was the harm in just one taste? One. No touching, just a kiss. A little tongue-tangling to set the mood.

The appreciation flaring to life in her eyes fed his

faulty justification, but with her gaze trailing over his body, and with more than a hint of desire there, as well, he sure didn't want to go out in public until he cooled his jets at least a small degree.

They were supposed to be a loving couple. The same loving couple half the staff was no doubt already whispering about being into kinky sex with video cameras and whipped cream. He hadn't missed the subtle lift of the bellman's eyebrow or the quick quirk of his mouth when he'd made the delivery to their room this afternoon. The newlyweds in Bungalow One had a reputation to uphold. Considering the state of his arousal, that shouldn't be a problem.

"Shall we go?" she asked, lifting a black lacy shawl from the bed to slip over her shoulders.

"Not just yet," he told her, and closed the space between them. His mind argued for him to stop, to respect her wishes and heed the warnings of distractions versus temptation. Too bad his body had an entirely different scenario in mind. "Something's missing."

She glanced down at her dress, then back at him, curiosity brimming in her lovely eyes. "You think?"

A slow grin tugged his lips. No, she didn't need anything else. What she had inside there already was pure perfection.

He lifted his hand and trailed his knuckles down the curve of her shoulder.

Curiosity fled, replaced by awareness as her eyes widened when he retraced the path. He slid his hand beneath the fall of her silky hair to cup the back of her neck.

"What do you think you're doing?" she said, her voice a sexy as sin, breathless whisper.

He smiled slowly. "Now what do you think?"

7

"I THINK you're about to break your promise," Ronnie said. Since pulling in her next breath took supreme effort and concentration, she was amazed her vocal cords even responded. Any thought of willing her racing heart to slow was next to impossible. And moving out of range of Blake's very kissable mouth was *so* not an option she wanted brought up for discussion.

She had to remain focused, though, especially since there was no earthly reason for him to kiss her. There was no bellman hovering around, nor other honeymooners for them to provide a convincing performance to, so why didn't she just say *no* and walk out the door?

Because she really wanted him to kiss her, that's why. The kind of kisses that would lead to pure pleasure. With a craving close to desperation, she wanted him to make her body hum with desire again. She didn't want to be an agent on an undercover assignment with the sexiest man alive. What she wanted was far more complicated for her...to simply be the woman he desired, to be completely and thoroughly made love to by a sensitive, attentive lover. To be wholly satisfied by Blake.

There had to be something seriously wrong with

her. She couldn't, wouldn't make the same mistake twice. Except the two men were worlds apart. It didn't help that she knew in her heart Blake was nothing like Trevor.

"I don't recall making an actual promise," he hedged, his voice a low sexy rumble that did nothing to squelch the slow uncurling of anticipation in her belly.

If she closed her eyes and waited for him to lower his head and nuzzle her neck, she'd be a goner. So why did she stupidly tip her head to the side in invitation? Why was she waiting for his warm breath to fan her sensitized skin? Because all those poised and ready nerve endings were just waiting to explode, to send electrifying little shockwaves through her.

She breathed in his delicious scent, and dutifully kept her eyes wide open. "We really should..." *Go,* but her vocal cords froze when his eyes darkened. He had that look, that look that said he was a heartbeat away from kissing her senseless.

He gave a brisk nod and turned toward the door. "I said that I understood you. And I promised to kiss you *only* when it was absolutely necessary."

As far as she was concerned, kissing Blake right this second was about as necessary as her next breath. He couldn't be thinking the same thing...could he? Was he being noble when he really wanted to...

It didn't matter. It *couldn't* matter. And she absolutely, positively, monumentally refused to make the same mistake twice. Dedication to the job had to remain her priority, and she was getting a little tired of having to constantly remind herself of that very important fact. History told her becoming intimately involved with her partner was professional suicide. She had goals, dammit, and they didn't include getting all hot and bothered over Blake.

To make sure her shaky resolve didn't crumble completely, she forced herself to pass through the door he held open for her, and stepped out into the warm sultry night. Putting much-needed physical space between them for the next few hours would be close to impossible, but she had to be strong for the sake of her sanity. "We have work to do, and we can't do it effectively if we allow ourselves to become distracted with..." *Sex!* "With other things," she said instead. Other more pleasurable things. Other wicked and naughty things.

She waited for him to close the door. "We didn't spend the afternoon exploring the city hoping to learn something about Clark or Seaport Manor just so we could lose sight of why we're really here."

He let out a sigh. Yeah, so she was preaching to the choir here, but she was right, and he darned well knew it. Even so, it didn't lessen her growing need for a different kind of exploration.

Pleasurable exploration. Wicked and naughty exploration.

He still hadn't heard back from his partner about Clark, not that they really expected to learn anything new. Clark was in the area on a regular basis for a reason, and the fact that he was making routine stops at Seaport Manor was just too much of a coincidence. As

Blake had reminded her during their sojourn as honeymooning tourists this afternoon, there were no coincidences when it came to the illegal drug trade. Something she knew more about than she was willing to admit.

"You're right about being distracted."

His admission made her heart start to flutter. Or was it because his hand rested on her back as they walked through the quiet village? Either way, it all spelled trouble with the letters *S-E-X.*

"We need to find a way to get close to Clark," he continued, "and until we can make contact with him, we shouldn't let ourselves become distracted."

"Exactly," she agreed, wishing he'd remove his hand. Instead of concentrating on the way his fingers lightly pressed against her back, she surveyed her surroundings. The path leading away from their bungalow was lit by white twinkle lights wrapped around palms and other leafy trees and shrubs she couldn't name. Soft, barely perceptible classical music was piped through speakers from somewhere in the shrubs. Whoever designed the honeymoon resort obviously held a master's in romantic settings.

"That doesn't mean I wouldn't appreciate being distracted," he said, "but perhaps at a more appropriate time."

And what, pray tell, would he consider a more appropriate time? Right about now could be very appropriate, if she'd let it happen. "I'm glad you agree," she told him, wondering when she'd become such a hypocrite.

"I don't. Not really," he admitted, "but it's what you want. So, until we bust this case open, it'll be strictly business. Okay?"

"Okay," she said, but her heart still managed a tiny flip in her chest at his admission. Did that mean if she told him she'd changed her mind, if she admitted that having sex would be a great way to pass the time when they weren't working, he'd agree? Goodness gracious, the temptation!

"Good," she said firmly, more to convince herself. "No sex."

He reached for her hand and stopped. "Who said anything about sex?" he asked when she looked up at him.

A nervous laugh escaped. He *hadn't* been talking about sex. But she sure had been *thinking* about sex. A lot. Could she be any more embarrassed? She didn't think so thanks to her Freudian slip. "Well, no one, but..." But possibilities were definitely intriguing.

"I was only going to suggest once we wrap up the case, maybe we could go out."

"Like on a date?" Why that surprised her, she couldn't exactly say. Maybe because her previous bad relationship hadn't exactly been what most folks would call traditional. A cup or two of coffee, or burger, fries and a soda while on surveillance in an unmarked car didn't qualify as a date. Come to think of it, she and Trevor had never actually dated. They worked, had sex, and worked some more. Oh sure, he romanced her, that was all part of his plan to seduce her into silence. Their interludes were reserved to his place or hers, and never in the traditional girl-gets-to-know-boy-while-dating sense.

That killer grin was back, the one that had the power to seduce her into just about anything…if she let it. "Sure. Why not?" he asked. He dropped his hand from her back to reach for her hand and lace their fingers together. "I kinda like your idea better though."

She struggled to ignore the delicious shockwaves rippling over her skin his touch and words evoked. Something that was fast becoming impossible to accomplish. "I'll take that as a compliment," she said. "But it wouldn't work. After we wrap up here, I'm returning to New York, then heading back to Savannah."

They turned right and left the more private areas surrounding the bungalows behind and stepped into a courtyard, complete with stone statues of Baroque design scattered around the perimeter. A few couples strolled around the large fountain dominating the courtyard, admiring the replica of Bernini's *Apollo and Daphne* in the center. The entire setting spelled more romance, in bright flashing neon.

"That sounds like a story worth hearing," he said.

"Maybe later," she hedged. She wasn't too keen on sharing her goals for the future with anyone just yet.

Instead of stopping to enjoy the ambience, Blake led them through the courtyard and down another narrow, curving path to the main section of the hotel. They passed through the cool, air-conditioned lobby and up a wide, curving flight of stairs to the upper level of the resort's main restaurant. Blake gave them his name and within moments they were seated at a table overlooking the moonlit Pacific.

According to McCall, Clark was due to make an appearance at the resort tonight. If she hadn't been so paranoid about spending time alone with Blake, they probably should have stayed in their room after all. At least there they had a view of the launches. Except as he'd suggested earlier that day, if they wanted to find out exactly what Clark was up to, then they'd need to get close to him. Something they couldn't do from their bungalow. With the video camera set up, if there was any movement near the launches, they'd get it on tape. Their goal tonight was to simply get out and mingle, and look for an opportunity to cozy up to their possible prime suspect.

Two hours later, after the most scrumptious seafood dinner Ronnie had ever had the pleasure of enjoying, she and Blake sat at a small table in the resort's main lounge, no closer to spotting their prey than they'd been when they arrived on the island that morning. Blake had chosen a table close to the wood-tiled dance floor that allowed them to keep an eye on the door. So far, nothing unusual had occurred, and Ronnie was starting to have doubts that Clark was even going to make an appearance.

She traced the rim of her wineglass with the tip of her finger and gazed into Blake's eyes. To anyone looking in their direction, they appeared to be completely absorbed in each other. Even she was having trouble remembering his display of attentiveness was strictly cover-related.

She glanced at her watch, then back at Blake. "Maybe we should have stayed in the room," she told him. "It's after eleven. I don't think he's going to show."

He reached for her hand and brought her fingers to his lips. "If he's here, he'll show," he said, applying a featherlight kiss to the back of her hand.

"You can't know that," she argued in a soft, intimate whisper only he could hear. "You said you'd never had any contact with the guy, so how would you even know?"

He shrugged. "I haven't, but I know his type. If he's anything like the bastard he used to run with, which I'm confident he is, he's going to show up tonight."

He turned her hand over and settled his mouth on the center of her palm. A flash of heat flew right to the pit of her belly the instant his tongue touched her skin. The inside of her thighs tingled and she pressed them together. Instead of cooling the heat settling there, she merely stoked the embers that'd been simmering all night. Maybe she should make use of the private lagoons—alone—and go for a swim to cool her heated body. At least it'd be more physically exhausting than the cold shower she was destined for tonight.

"From what we know," she managed, "Clark flies just under the radar where no one can detect him. Coming here doesn't make sense, especially if he's involved like you suspect."

He took her hand and brought it to his neck, then

leaned forward. His mouth hovered inches above hers. She couldn't bear another kiss. Not without completely losing her sanity.

"Guys like Clark," he said in a low voice, "the ones who skate away time and again, the ones we can never seem to pin anything on, like to think they're untouchable. It's usually their downfall. How long have you suspected Seaport?"

She couldn't have torn her gaze away from his mouth if her life depended on it. "A little over two months, maybe closer to three."

He placed his finger under her chin, urging her to look away from the erotic danger zone of his mouth. "And in all that time," he said, a knowing light entering his eyes, "no one has ever connected him to this place, have they?"

She shook her head because her vocal cords stopped working the second she looked into his gray eyes. The darkening of his gaze added to her already overloaded senses and doubled her confusion. The lines of professionalism had gone from blurred to nonexistent. She no longer cared whether or not this seduction act was real. She wanted Blake, and to hell with the consequences.

"According to McCall," he continued, as if he wasn't sending her senses into a tailspin, "the visits to Seaport every ten days are a recent development, am I right?"

At least one of them was able to keep their mind on the case. All she could do was nod mutely in response.

"Clark's going to get sloppy. We've got a pattern

here, Ronnie. You can't sit there and tell me you don't see it."

She managed another nod in agreement.

"Clark's recent activity indicates he feels he's not only above the law, but smarter than the rest of us, and his routine trips to Seaport means he's rubbing our noses in it."

Focus, dammit, focus. Unfortunately, it was something she simply could not accomplish as long as Blake was touching her, or talking to her in that sexy, pillow-talk voice.

"Possibly," she said, pulling away from him. She had to, or she'd do something really stupid, like loop her arms around his neck and attack. "It still doesn't prove anything, though. As far as anyone has been able to tell, this guy is clean. There's no reason to even suspect him. If it wasn't for your knowledge of Clark, I doubt we'd treat him any differently than any other suspect. And, once we learned that he was clean, we might not have even bothered with surveillance."

He obviously didn't take the hint, because he settled his hand on her knee. She nearly jumped out of her chair.

"Not with McCall noticing the pattern. Patterns are red flags in any investigation, you know that."

No more of a red flag than the one Blake kept waving in front of her. Like the kind a matador uses to tease a bull into an angry charge. Except this one taunted and teased her with seduction in the form of the lazy pattern he was drawing with his thumb over her knee.

"Eventually," he continued, "the information could've made it into the file and someone might've picked up on it. We just got ourselves a head start because I happened to have heard of the guy."

Something he said snagged her attention, and she momentarily forgot about the way her skin tingled. Heard of the guy?

She put her hand over Blake's and removed his long, warm fingers from her knee. "Are you saying you don't have a clue what this guy looks like?"

He silence spoke volumes.

"Blake? Please tell me you've at least seen him before."

"Not exactly."

"We could be seated next to him and not know it?"

"We'll know him, Ronnie."

She wasn't reassured. "How? It's not like he'll have a sign hanging around his neck that says, 'I'm a drug lord, bust me.'"

For the last three hours she'd been tortured by Blake's touch, by his nearness, by the desire brimming in his eyes, and for what? She'd been reminding herself over and over again how getting involved with him on a personal level was nothing short of professional suicide, and struggled all night with keeping her head in the job. She'd been under the mistaken impression he knew Alister Clark on sight. She hadn't thought to pose the question earlier, because the thought that they'd spend three hours waiting for someone that he couldn't even identify was ludicrous.

She pushed her chair back and stood.

"Where are you going?"

"To the Sunset Bar."

"Ronnie—"

She really wanted to tell him to go back to their room. She could handle things from here, but she couldn't afford the luxury of raising suspicion by being alone in a bar on her supposed honeymoon. Stuck. That's what she was—stuck with a partner that turned her inside out and didn't even know what their suspect looked like.

With a sigh, she snagged her black-satin evening bag from the table. "Are you coming?"

"Anything the lady wants," he said with a grin, seemingly immune to her snit.

Boy, was that a loaded lead-in if she ever heard one. "What the lady wants right this minute is something we're both better off ignoring."

BLAKE SURVEYED THE occupants of the Sunset Bar and waited for Ronnie to be seated. "I don't see him."

She made a sound that could have been a laugh, but sounded a lot more like an unladylike display of disgust. "How would you know?"

He gave her a tolerant look and took the chair next to her instead of across the table, as he suspected would make her more comfortable. "I was referring to McCall," he said patiently.

She scooted her chair a few inches away and he smiled. He'd made a decision, one that was far from intelligent and eons away from wise, but he wanted Ronnie. She'd been twisting him in knots since she'd walked into Forbes's office, and from her reaction to him all day and into the night, he'd wager his pension she wanted him, too. Something was holding her back, and he assumed it was a combination of her sense of duty to the job and her previous bad experience.

"Considering his shift started early in the afternoon, I could've told you he wouldn't be here at this hour," she said, adjusting the hem of her little black dress. She pulled her wrap a little higher on her shoulders to ward off the chill of the evening sea breeze. Leaning back in her chair, she crossed her legs, giving him a great view of all that nylon-clad skin that could easily drive a man to his knees.

"So what do you suggest we do now?" He had his own plans, and they included heavy-duty flirtation in an attempt to scale that damned wall she kept trying to keep between them.

"We'll order a drink and see what develops," she said, and stood.

He snagged her hand before she had a chance to take off toward the bar. "Uh-uh. I'll go."

She let out a sigh that was more of a frustrated puff of air and sat down again. "What difference does it make?"

"See that guy over there?" he indicated with a brief nod of his head. "The one sitting at the far end of the bar?"

She pulled her hand from his grasp before she looked in the direction he indicated. "Yeah. So?"

"So, how do you know that's not Clark?"

"I don't. Not for certain, but it's my guess that is not the man we're looking for."

"Why?"

She shrugged. "Simple. The cheap suit. Our guy is a high roller, who probably wouldn't be caught dead in anything less than Armani."

Her instincts impressed him. "What about that guy? The one at the table in the far corner eyeing the waitress."

She smiled, and his heart did a funny flip in his chest. "Way too old," she said.

"Old?" he scoffed. "You think mid-thirties is old?"

"Not him," she said, her voice filled with humor. "His wife. Clark's wife, if he even has one, is probably some Barbie Doll bimbo."

Blake agreed. There'd be no May-December romance for someone like Alister Clark. Ronnie was right. Arm candy would be more his speed.

She shifted in her chair to get a better look around the outdoor bar. "This is worse than trying to find a contact lens in a dark theater."

"Let's call it a night and start fresh tomorrow," he suggested. "We aren't even certain he's arrived."

She turned back to face him, a wry grin curving her mouth. "Or what he looks like," she said, a teasing light entering her turquoise eyes. "Maybe we should wait until we can contact McCall or Anderson. At least then McCall could give us a description."

Blake moved to stand, but stilled midway when he spied a distinguished-looking gentleman coming up the wooden steps to the bar. "The night is young after all," he said, returning to his seat. "Over there, walking toward the bar."

Ronnie scooted her chair nearer his, then leaned close. With her hand resting over his, she asked quietly, "Are you sure it's him?"

He laced their fingers together. All his instincts went on full alert. "Not one-hundred percent," he told her, but he was pretty positive they'd just spotted their suspect. "He's somebody, though, that's for sure. Check out the bartender. He's breaking his neck to get to the guy."

She squeezed his hand. For reassurance? he wondered, when she pulled her hand from his.

She pushed her chair away from the table. "I'm going to the bar," she said.

"No, you're not." Watching Clark from across the deck was one thing, but he wasn't about to let Ronnie walk up to him. Not alone.

She gave him an impatient glance. "We have to find out if it's him, Blake. Do you really want to waste the next couple of days tailing this man if he's not our guy?"

Blake looked back toward the bar. The man in question couldn't be more than forty, forty-five tops, which put him around the right age. He had light brown hair, cut short, but stylish. His clothes were the highest quality, obviously tailor-made. No off-the-rack for this guy. "It's him, Ronnie. I can feel it."

"We have to be sure. I'm going to the bar." She eased out of her chair and stood.

"Don't do it, Ronnie," he warned.

"Don't worry, I won't do anything to put the case in jeopardy. Just sit back and watch a pro in action, *babe*."

He didn't think she'd put herself or the case in danger, but that didn't mean he wouldn't stop her if necessary. If he tried now, they'd make a scene and draw unwanted attention to themselves. Besides, she certainly wasn't about to ask for ID then arrest the guy if it was Clark. For one, they didn't have anything on him, except suspicion fueled by a hunch. Blake always trusted his hunches.

With nothing else for him to do but watch, wait and be ready to spring into action if necessary, he forced himself to sit back in the padded patio chair and appear relaxed. Ronnie walked straight to where Clark was sitting on a bar stool and sidled up to the bar.

Blake stiffened, but she ignored Clark. Clark however, failed to return the favor. He glanced in Ronnie's direction, then did a double take. Not that Blake could blame the guy, but he didn't like the creep ogling his woman.

His *partner*, he silently amended. The correction, and reminder, did nothing to lessen the sharp twist in his gut, nor the fierce need to protect Ronnie. Partners looked out for each other. Unfortunately, he had a bad feeling their relationship skipped right over the line of standard partnership and into foreign territory.

Still, she was one hot little number in that figure-hugging black dress, and Clark obviously had no qualms about appreciating the sight of a beautiful woman. She was close enough to the guy for him to breathe in her intoxicating scent, too.

Blake's hands tightened on the arms of the chair.

The bartender finally made his way down the bar to Ronnie to place her order. The bartender said something to the guy next to her, and if Blake hadn't been watching her closely, he might have missed the slight stiffening in her shoulders.

This was it. They had their guy.

Suddenly, he couldn't breathe. It scared the hell out of him that Ronnie was inches from Clark. Not the kind of reaction a seasoned detective should be having, he thought, but that didn't stop him from struggling for air as Ronnie continued to ignore Clark while she waited for the bartender to deliver her order.

The bartender set two drinks on the bar in front of her, and she waited again until he returned with a charge slip. She signed it, picked up the two glasses of wine and turned, dumping the wine onto Alister Clark's lap.

8

RONNIE GASPED appropriately and quickly set the now empty glasses on the bar to reach for a stack of cocktail napkins. "I am so sorry," she said, as she began swiping at the wine she'd intentionally spilled on Clark.

"It's okay," he said calmly, taking the napkins from her. "Accidents happen."

She offered her sweetest smile. "This is completely my fault," she told him, hoping he couldn't see through her saccharine routine. "Silly me, I wasn't paying attention."

Much to her relief, he smiled down at her as if to set her at ease. He did have a nice smile, even if he was a suspected drug smuggler, and intense blue eyes she safely assumed took in everything around him.

"There's no need to concern yourself," he said kindly, taking more dry napkins from the holder.

She managed a nervous-sounding laugh and handed a few more cocktail napkins to him. She couldn't believe their incredible luck, to have actually made contact with Clark on their first night out. With any luck, she and Blake would be wrapping up the case in a day or two and she'd be taking the steps necessary to lead her own life. "I'm not usually so clumsy. I promise to pay for the cleaning."

"That's not necessary," he said, his deep, smooth voice showing no signs of impatience. He signaled for the bartender, who immediately left what he was doing to attend to Clark. "Two more of whatever the lady just ordered."

"Right away, Mr. Clark."

Judging from the bartender's swiftness, it was obvious Alister Clark got what he wanted, when he wanted, telling Ronnie loud and clear the man was either a regular patron at the resort or, as Blake believed, somehow connected to the resort on a more personal level. Maybe buried under a series of dummy corporations? She was beginning to think it highly possible.

"I really do insist on paying for the cleaning," she said, trying to determine what her next move should be. Thanks to McCall, they knew Clark would be in the area for at least a few days, which wasn't all that long considering they needed to find out if he was involved in the smuggling. "Do you have a card? I'll put my room number on it so you can have the bill sent to me."

"Don't think twice about it." He settled his hand on her arm and squeezed ever so gently. His touch was cool, his hands smooth, not at all calloused. She thought of a snake, one of those big, thick ones that strangled its prey, and she very nearly cringed at the touch.

"Ronnie, honey? Is everything okay?"

She let out a sigh at the sound of Blake's voice. Not

one of relief, she told herself firmly. After all, she was used to the Alister Clarks of the world.

She turned and smiled at her partner. "Just my usual clumsy self," she said, throwing in another nervous laugh for effect. "This is...I'm sorry, what did you say your name was?"

"Clark," he said, reaching to shake Blake's hand. "Alister Clark."

The two men shook hands. "Blake St. Claire," Blake offered cordially.

They needed to find out what Clark was up to. Was he involved with Seaport Manor? Why did he keep returning to the resort every ten days? And what did he do when he was here?

Determined to find answers, she wasn't about to walk away until she learned at least something about the man. Something she could give to her superiors to run through the computers. Some piece of information that could link Clark to the resort. "Will you at least allow me to buy you a fresh drink?" she asked him.

He shifted his attention from Blake to her. His gaze quickly scanned the length of her, but it was so brief, she had a hard time finding any self-righteous indignation.

"Only if you'll join me...was it Ronnie?"

"Yes. It's a nickname. Veronica Car...excuse me. St. Claire." The bubble of laughter sounded nervous, and felt a little too real thanks to her near slip. "It's still a little new to me."

She climbed onto the vacant bar stool, ignoring Blake's warning glance. She wasn't about to blow their big chance now that she had Clark engaged in conversation. Hopefully, before the evening ended they'd have something that could land them a possible lead or at least a hint that solid evidence existed.

Clark nodded his dark-blond head in thanks to the bartender when he returned with two fresh glasses of wine. "Honeymooning?"

She laid her black-silk purse on the bar and crossed her legs. "If you can call it that. There's really not much to do here, is there? I wanted to see Europe again, but Blake," she said, reaching for her partner's hand, "insisted he couldn't be away from his precious brokerage firm for too long."

Clark eyed Blake curiously and her hope soared. "You're in the investment business?"

Ronnie sighed. "Not a very interesting *hobby* if you ask me." God, she hated playing the bored airheaded wife, but as far as she could tell, it was working. Clark was talking to them, and now really showing interest.

Blake had to give Ronnie credit. The bored socialite routine was close to perfection, and just enough to pique Clark's curiosity without being overdone. He had a feeling Clark's interest went beyond Ronnie's mention of finances, though, if the way Clark's gaze kept dipping to Ronnie's cleavage was any indication.

"Now, sweetheart," Blake said, using a patient, near condescending tone, "how many times do I have to tell you? It's not just a hobby."

She shrugged and waved her hand in dismissal. "Well, it all seems silly to me," she said airily. "Especially when he has a legion of financial advisors already. Why he has to play around with all that dirty money himself is just beyond my little ol' realm of comprehension."

If she wanted to play the dingbat, then who was he to argue. Especially when it appeared to be working based on the understanding look Clark sent his way.

Blake took the wineglass Ronnie offered. "What I can't seem to make my wife understand is that the right kind of investment can be very exciting. Don't you agree, Mr. Clark?"

A shrewd light entered Clark's eyes. "Yes, indeed. Very exciting."

Ronnie took a sip from her own glass. "You dabble in investments, too? Must be a guy thing."

Oh, she's good, Blake thought, and smothered a grin. She had Alister Clark eating out of her hand with this dingy Southern belle act.

The sly smile Clark bestowed on Ronnie was just shy of condescending. "In the business of making money, Mrs. St. Claire," he said, "it's anyone's thing."

"I find it boring. Blake claims the benefits can be very rewarding. And he does get so excited when he can find a way to keep the IRS's grubby hands off of his money. Don't you, darling?"

Okay, she was starting to go just a little too far, in his opinion. They couldn't be too obvious or Clark might get suspicious. "Sugar, you're going to bore Mr. Clark," he said, hoping she caught his warning glance.

"Oh, nonsense, Blake," she said impatiently. "I'm sure Mr. Clark would love to discuss all those boring investments and figures with you. Especially if it's his thing, too."

He knew what she was up to, but she was beginning to lay it on a little too thick. They had to be careful not to raise suspicion.

"Sweetheart," he said a little forcefully. "Surely that lovely finishing school taught you that it's impolite to discuss financial matters in public."

She narrowed her eyes at him, then flashed Clark one of her hundred-watt smiles. "My husband is right," she said. "Forgive me for being so rude."

Clark patted Ronnie's hand. "There's no need to apologize, Mrs. St. Claire. I admit to finding the discussion very fascinating indeed."

Blake had a feeling money was the last thing Clark was referring to, considering he couldn't seem to keep his hands off Ronnie. He didn't like it, not one bit. It didn't help that Ronnie was a pro at flirting, either.

This was not the way he'd envisioned their investigation. They were originally sent in to find out who was operating behind the scenes. Blake knew in his gut Clark was involved somehow, and while he'd originally been the one to suggest they find a way to get close to him, he'd be the first to admit he might've been wrong for the simple reason he didn't like Ronnie anywhere near this guy.

Blake reached between Ronnie and Clark to set his still-full wineglass on the bar. He looked directly at Ronnie so she'd have no doubt he was calling a halt to the evening's activities. "We really should be going. We have an early day tomorrow."

She arched one eyebrow. "We do?"

Blake frowned. "You said you wanted to do some more shopping."

She laughed, but the look in her eyes was anything but humorous. "Darling, we saw about everything there was to see here today. We really should have done Europe like I wanted. At least then we could have attended a few parties. You know, liven things up a bit."

Clark stood suddenly. "I'm having a small get-together aboard the *Mary Alice* tomorrow," he said, directing his comments to Ronnie. "Just a few close friends. Nothing quite as exciting as I'm sure you're looking for, but I'd love to have you."

Blake just bet Clark would love to have her. Well, not on his watch. As far as he was concerned, he wasn't about to let Ronnie out of his sight when Clark was around. Not only was he a dangerous son-of-a-bitch, Blake was having a hard time getting past the looks Clark kept tossing in Ronnie's direction.

"The *Mary Alice?*" she asked with feigned innocence.

"My yacht. She's anchored offshore. I'll have someone pick you up, say around noon at the main launch?"

Blake felt as if he was on a runaway train and the brake just fell off into his hand. "I don't think we—"

"We'd love to," Ronnie interrupted him. "It's been ages since I've been sailing."

This was her job, he rationalized. Ronnie was no rookie, and of course, realized she was putting them both in a potentially volatile situation by agreeing to walk right into the wolf's den. However reluctantly, he was damned impressed with her progress and how she'd managed to turn their first contact with Clark into a golden opportunity.

"It's a date then," Clark said. "I should be going. My wife will wonder what's become of me."

They said their goodbyes, and Blake waited until Clark disappeared before he snagged Ronnie's hand and urged her from the bar stool.

"That went extremely well, don't you think?" she asked, once they were out of the Sunset Bar.

Blake gave her hand a squeeze. "Okay, I'll admit it. You impressed me. Although I did think the airhead routine was a bit much."

She laughed, the sound as light and airy as the gentle breeze coming in from the Pacific. "Why thank you, sir," she said, using the same thick accent she'd used on Clark.

"Don't thank me yet," he said, as he guided her through the courtyard and onto the lighted path that would take them back to their bungalow. Where they would be alone. Just the two of them...and a king-size bed they'd be sharing soon. "Do you have a plan in mind?"

They walked into their own private patio. "Search the yacht, of course," she said, and took the room key from him.

"And you expect to find what?" he asked as she opened the door. "White bags of synthetic powder stacked topside just waiting to be picked up by whoever Clark is involved with on this deal?"

"Don't be ridiculous," she said, pushing the door open.

He followed her inside. "You know, there is always the possibility Clark could be as suspicious of us as we are of him."

"I don't know what your problem is," she said, tossing her lace wrap on one of the Queen Anne chairs, "but I'm starting to get the feeling you're not too excited about tomorrow."

He pulled in a deep breath, and let it out slow, but it did zilch to ease the tension that started to creep up the back of his neck. "That's not what I'm saying. I just want you to be careful."

There, he'd said it. Be careful. Don't get hurt. Don't take chances. He tried to tell himself it was nothing more than he'd say to Luke, but he had a bad feeling there was more involved here. A whole lot more, and that had him worried there was something deeper, something way too personal regarding his feelings for Ronnie than a mere temporary partnership.

She kicked off her shoes. "I am a seasoned undercover operative," she told him, reaching up to remove her earrings next. "I've handled men like Alister Clark before."

He moved to the edge of the bed and sat before rubbing at the knot in the back of his neck. "I know you have."

She set her earrings on the top of the dresser, and

turned to face him. "Then what's wrong, Blake? Something is bothering you. Now what is it?"

"I know it's our job, but I don't like the thought of you being that close to Clark. It spooks me, okay?"

She walked to the bed and sat, then took his hand and held it in her own. It'd be so easy to turn, to cup the warmth of her cheek in his palm and kiss her senseless.

"That's very sweet of you," she said, "and I do appreciate your concern. But, Blake, I *can* handle Alister Clark. This might not be how I want to make my living, but as long as I'm wearing a badge, I'll do my job and I'll do it well."

With his hand still clasped in hers, he looked at her as if really seeing her for the first time. There were so many things about Ronnie he didn't know, and he was damned certain he could spend the rest of his life with her and never completely understand her. For everything he knew, there were many more facets to her personality that remained a mystery.

Good thing he was great at solving mysteries.

"What do you want?" he asked. Was he referring to her career goals, or something much more personal?

She shook her head. "It's not important."

He begged to differ. "I think it is. We're about to head off in a very dangerous direction. If your heart's not in what we're facing tomorrow, then I think we should call it off and find another way to approach the case."

She pulled her hand from his, but remained seated beside him. "You have nothing to worry about. I am more than ready for whatever happens tomorrow. I need to solve this case. It's going to be my last if we manage an arrest."

He grinned. "Retirement? At the ripe old age of what? Twenty-eight?"

"No," she said with a hint of gentle laughter in her voice. "I'm looking at a career change is all."

"Let me guess. A lawyer."

She laughed. "Not even close. Actually, I plan to start my own business. That's why I'm moving back to Savannah."

"A bed-and-breakfast then? Carmichael's Crash Pad."

"Don't ever take up advertising for a living, okay? I would hate to have to worry that you're starving to death."

He returned her mischievous grin. "Come on, Ronnie. What is it?"

"Nope." She shook her head. "Can we change the subject please?"

"Not until you tell me."

She sighed dramatically and turned to look at him. Her eyes sparkled and the smile curving her lips made his mouth water. "Okay, but be warned. One laugh and I'll have to shoot you or something."

When he nodded, she pulled in a deep breath and let it out along with a rush of words. "A gift and collectibles boutique."

He didn't laugh, but he did smile and reach for her hand.

"I mean it," she warned. "Don't you dare laugh."

"Now why would I do that?" he asked, guiding her back to the bed again.

"I don't know," she said, fiddling with the hem of her dress.

"Maybe because retail is a hell of a long way from drug busts," he offered.

"My point exactly. I never wanted a career in law enforcement. But when my brother was killed by a drunk driver, everyone in my family just sort of assumed I would fill the void."

"I'm sorry about your brother."

"Thank you."

"Even so, that's a pretty large assumption."

"There hasn't been a generation of Carmichaels that hasn't worn a badge of some sort."

"You don't have to explain. I understand." And he did. He'd never wanted to be anything else. The main difference was that he'd wanted to be like his old man, at least as far as wearing a badge. As a father and husband, Jim Hammond left a whole lot to be desired, but when it came to being a cop, his dad had been one of the best.

He let out a sigh and stood. "We should probably do some surveillance before going aboard Clark's yacht tomorrow," he said, changing the subject.

She grinned suddenly. "You want surveillance? We've got surveillance," she said coming off the bed.

She crossed the room to the video camera and pulled the tape, replacing it with a new one, then reset the camera to record. She held the small 8 mm recorded tape between her thumb and index finger.

"Clark as much as admitted he uses the main launch. Maybe we got lucky twice in one night."

"You think you're going to have him moving drugs on that tape? I wouldn't count on it, Ronnie."

She bent to pull a case from the black bag on the chair next to the camera so they could play the tape on the VCR. He struggled for air at the sight of the outline of her delectable backside pressing against the silk of her dress.

"What makes you say that?" she asked. She bent over farther as she riffled through the bag, causing her dress to climb higher and exposing the lacy tops of her stockings. He was dead certain his heart stopped beating. "You were the one who suspected he was involved."

He swallowed. Hard. "Involved, yes," he managed, despite the narrowing of his air passages. "Clark's not stupid. You don't seriously believe we'll get him moving the drugs himself, do you?"

She straightened and padded across the thick carpet in her stocking feet, only to bend over again and cause his heart rate to speed up to double time. "There's only one way to find out for certain," she told him as she slipped the cassette into the VCR.

She found the remote and hit the play button. After a few seconds of gray-and-white snow, the scene outside their window came onto the screen. Because of the breakers, only gentle waves lapped against the shore. The launch was deserted with the exception of the docking of two of Seaport Manor's water taxis. The only other movement came from the slight swaying of palms from the constant sea breeze that blew across the island.

"We've got over four hours recorded," he said. "This could take all night." He checked his watch; it was past midnight. "I don't know about you, but I'm beat. It's been a long day."

She gave him an impatient look, then hit the fast forward button. Less than five minutes later, a movement to the right of the screen caught his attention.

"Whoa. Back up a minute."

"I saw it," she said, and rewound the tape. "There."

She hit Play and together they watched the tape closely. Something moved on the lower half of the screen. He couldn't quite make out the images on the television so he leaned forward and strained to get a better look.

She made a sound that sounded like a combination of a strangled laugh and a cough. "Oh, my."

Then he saw it, the tangled limbs of a man and woman, half hidden by palm fronds. There was no mistaking what the couple was doing as the man eased the woman's legs over his shoulders before he dipped his head and began to make love to her with his mouth. Blake couldn't see the woman's face or hear her cries of ecstasy, but that didn't stop his own imagination from running wild as the couple made love in what they thought was a private moment right there on the beach.

Ronnie knew she should turn off the tape, or at the very least, hit the fast forward button, but she was mesmerized by the act of love being played out on the screen. The image of Blake's mouth on her, drawing out all her intimate secrets, floated through her mind. When the man's hands gripped the woman's thighs and urged her to open more for him, it was Blake's hands on her, loving her, carrying her over the precipice into sensual oblivion. Taking her to that place where only need and desire existed, where fulfillment meant more than the next breath.

Her breathing became heavy. She felt hot. Achy. Needy. Maybe she should be ashamed for becoming aroused by watching such a personal, intimate act, but she could find no shame in what the couple was doing. There was no humility whatsoever in the way her own body craved Blake's touch, no matter how foolhardy acting out the fantasies running through her mind would be to her resolve never to fall victim to another sweet-talking, irresistible charmer with a sexy-as-sin smile.

She cast a surreptitious glance in his direction only to find him equally mesmerized by the act of love that had been captured on video. Were his thoughts traveling down the same dangerous path as her own? Was he imagining what it would be like to touch her, to kiss her so intimately, to bring their bodies together toward the ultimate satisfaction?

Her gaze dipped to his trousers and she held back a needy groan. There was no mistaking the erection pressing against the silk material. Her awareness of Blake, and her own need, heightened to the point where rational thought was in danger of slipping away and physical pleasure ruled her mind, her body and, dammit, her heart, too.

She couldn't take another minute of this and promptly pressed the stop button on the remote control. A cold shower would never suffice. She needed activity, physical activity to burn off the sharp heated edge of desire and need simmering inside her.

She pushed off the bed, slipped into her shoes and snagged her room key from the top of the dresser.

"Where are you going?" he asked. His voice sounded as taut as she felt at the moment.

"For a swim," she managed by the time she reached the door. And hopefully some peace of mind and perspective.

"Without a suit?" he asked. The tortured note in his voice made him sound as though he was being strangled.

"With any luck, the private lagoons won't be in use this time of night," she said, and slipped through the door into the night air that did nothing to cool her heated skin.

One thought slipped into her mind as she crossed the courtyard. Regardless of her previous experience with her former partner, regardless of how dangerous it would be for her heart to become intimately involved with Blake, she knew deep in her soul he was everything he seemed. He was honest, loyal to his partner and the badge, and the fact that he was concerned for her welfare was as close to the breaking point as she could get. There wasn't a single shred of dishonesty in Blake Hammond's incredible body.

Whether or not that made it acceptable for her to forget her own vow never to become involved with law-enforcement types, let alone her own temporary partner, she couldn't say. Nor did she want to analyze the situation too deeply, because as she made her way along the deserted, winding path to the private lagoons, she couldn't help wondering if she'd just unconsciously handed Blake an engraved invitation to join her.

9

BLAKE STOOD before the last door to the private lagoons. The first two were deserted. He hadn't followed Ronnie because he knew she'd be all wet and naked, or because he'd been as turned on as her, thanks to their unexpected journey into voyeurism courtesy of the surveillance video. At least that's what he kept trying to tell himself, arguing instead with his conscience that he'd followed her strictly for her protection. Which was damned laughable considering Ronnie was a trained professional and could probably take him down given the opportunity.

So why was he here if it wasn't to protect a woman who needed no protection? Certainly not something as simple, or as complicated, as lust. He'd certainly been experiencing it by the truckload, and it definitely explained why he'd followed her to the lagoons. Arguing otherwise was a waste of energy, he realized. Besides, wasn't it about time they both faced the truth? He wanted Ronnie. Period. And he'd bet his precious fourteen days of vacation she wanted him just as much.

If she told him to leave, naturally he'd respect her wishes, but his instincts told him she'd welcome his presence...and not just to keep her company while she went for a midnight swim.

The thought of her skinny-dipping, of her smooth, golden skin being caressed by the cool water had him placing his hand on the doorknob before his common sense could overrule his lust.

He pushed open the door and walked through to the other side, then closed it quietly behind him and turned the lock to ensure their privacy.

The area was lit only by the moonlight filtering through the domed skylight and by small lamps set within the rock and foliage-covered walls. Thin beams of soft light added to the romantic ambience, as did the easy jazz playing on the stereo system hidden behind the cabinet doors they'd explored earlier that day. Over the sound of water running down the rocks into the pool, he recognized the soulful melodies of Kenny G.

Steam rose from the pool, making the air inside the lagoon warm and humid despite the controlled temperature. Already the silk of his trousers felt as heavy as wool against his skin. He waited, listening for some sound of her presence, but other than the music and the rush of water from the man-made waterfall, the room was silent.

And then he heard it, a sound by the waterfall that was so whisper-soft he wondered if his common sense had risen in the nick of time.

"You're a mistake, Blake."

Not exactly an invitation, nor was it a demand for him to leave, either. Something in between, he guessed. As though she was allowing him the final decision about whether or not he should stay and make love to her. If he stayed, that's exactly what was going to happen. Now that he was here, he had no misconceptions about why he'd followed her in the first place. But if she took herself out of the decision-making equation, did it mean she was looking to absolve herself of responsibility? By not making that choice herself, would it leave her with no guilt? No regrets, and only pleasure?

Pleasure he could provide. Absolution had to be hers.

Guided by the subdued lighting, he crossed the sandy floor to the chaise and kicked his shoes off next to hers. Either she'd been expecting him or hoping he'd follow. From the cabinet she'd also retrieved two large fluffy towels and the small supply of condoms. The only item missing was a silver ice bucket with chilled champagne.

Turning to face the water, he pulled his socks off next as he searched the semidarkness for her. All he could make out was her silhouette against the waterfall. "Some mistakes don't have anywhere near the repercussions you think they will," he told her.

"How do you know?"

He shrugged out of his tie and dress shirt and laid them on the chaise with her dress. His stomach bottomed out when he spied her black, strapless bra and lacy panties peeking out from under the silky material of her dress. Imagining her swimming in the nude and waiting for him was one thing. Reality had him struggling for air.

"You don't," he managed around the sudden dryness of his throat. "At least not until it's over."

She laughed, the sound low and throaty, and sexy as hell. "By then it's too late."

"What are you afraid of?" If he could set her fears aside, he would, but he had a feeling whatever it was that was causing her hesitation, she'd have to figure it out for herself. He only hoped she did so soon. The sight of those condoms, along with the sound of her sultry voice was a turn-on of epic proportions.

"Repeating history," she said after a moment.

"That's what we do, Ronnie. Human beings have been repeating history since the beginning of time. How else do you explain war?"

She laughed again. "Remind me not to come to you for comfort."

"Is it comfort you really want?" he asked, sliding his hands into the pockets of his slacks. "Or something much more powerful? And pleasurable."

He heard her sharp intake of breath and his own pulse picked up speed. A thousand varieties of pleasure would only be the beginning.

"Why can't I have all three?" she asked.

He'd give her three dozen of whatever she wanted, if she let him. "You can. But only if you're willing to let go and enjoy the moment for what it is."

"The moment, huh?" A small splash of water and she disappeared beneath the surface.

He remained standing, barefoot in the sand, still

wearing his trousers, waiting for her to reappear and give him a signal she truly wanted him to stay.

She resurfaced near him, and rose from the pool. Walking toward him, she wore nothing but a sweet, seductive smile. Miles of smooth golden skin glistened in the moonlight. As she neared, he watched, mesmerized, as tiny rivulets of water seemed to pulse down her body and along her curves to fall at her feet. He nearly forgot to breathe. God, she was so beautiful.

"Are you sure about this?" he asked her. The sound of his heart beat loudly in his ears as the seconds seemed suspended while he waited for her answer.

Her smile widened. "How very noble of you, Blake."

Noble was the last thing he was feeling. Sexually charged. Hot. Aching. Aching for her. Any one of a dozen adjectives applied, and they all came down to one thing...he had to have her. "Not so noble," he admitted. "More like if we start, I don't know if I can stop."

She narrowed the distance between them. "Then maybe," she said, smoothing her hand over his chest, "we should concentrate on the moment."

He laid his hand on hers, trapping her palm over his heart, certain she could feel the frantic rhythm beating beneath his chest. "I want nothing more," he said, looking down into her brilliant gaze. "But I need you to be absolutely sure this is what you want, Ronnie. If you're not in this completely, tell me now and I'll go back to the bungalow and we can pretend this night never happened."

It might kill him to do it, but he meant every word. He'd walk away if she wasn't willing to give herself to him one hundred percent. He wasn't asking for forever. He wasn't even asking for tomorrow or the day after that. He knew she had dragons hiding behind the gate, pale as they might or might not seem in the light of day. All she wanted, all she could offer him, was now, and he accepted her terms, knowing that his doing so made her feel safer. If that was the case, so be it, so long as it meant bringing all the awareness that'd been simmering between them for the last forty-eight hours to a culmination of pleasure and satisfaction.

"Just the moment," he said. "Only now. Only tonight. With no regrets."

She reached for his free hand and brought it to her breast. "For the moment," she whispered.

He cupped her damp, cool flesh. The weight of her breast in his palm, the touch of her soft skin against his fingers, combined with her hand splayed over his, holding him against her heart, was more erotic than he could have ever imagined possible. "This is going to be a moment neither one of us will soon forget," he said, then released her hand to wrap his arm around her slender waist and pull her closer. She molded to his body, her curves pressing enticingly against him. He lowered his head to capture her sweet lips in a kiss he foolishly imagined would begin as a tender, gentle exploration. Instead he was greeted with instant heat and fire.

Ronnie knew she was repeating history to some degree. She even believed she was, on some level, making a huge mistake. Except she could wrest no objection strong enough that would pull her from Blake's arms and the glorious sensations coursing through her body.

She wanted him. Since the moment she first challenged him in Lieutenant Forbes's office, she'd wanted him. Admitting the attraction hadn't been easy, but the sparks between them were too electrical and powerful to ignore for long.

She needed him. Needed him to soothe the ache within her, along with the restlessness that had been her constant companion since she'd met him, a restlessness she knew deep in her heart only his touch could calm.

The reality of it frightened her as much as it fascinated her. Beneath the heat, beneath the passion that had been simmering from day one, there was one simple truth—the honesty of making love. With Blake, there were no false promises. No lies and no dishonesty involved. This time there was only need and pleasure and the heady promise of fulfillment.

If she had any regrets, they stemmed from her not being able to ask Blake to leave. The minute she heard the click of the door when he'd closed it, she'd known they would make love. Inevitability was something she found tough to argue, especially now when she realized that every second they'd spent together had been leading up to this very moment.

She wreathed her arms around his neck and pressed closer, loving the feel of his hard, warm body against hers. The silk of his trousers rasped against her bare legs, adding more delicious sensations to her already overloaded senses. His scent, the beat of his heart, the warmth of his skin, all fed the hunger inside. Her skin tingled. Her toes curled. Her center grew moist with need.

She shifted her position so her legs straddled his thigh, then she rocked her hips forward. The feel of his silk slacks against her most intimate place had her issuing a moan of frustration mingled with pleasure. She wanted him naked, to feel the full hard contours of his body pressed against her softness. To feel the friction of skin against skin, heat against heat, man against woman in the most elemental way possible.

Lifting her knee, she rubbed the inside of his thigh, going as high as she could manage without losing her balance. She teased his penis, which was straining against his zipper, and he made a sound deep in his throat. One large warm hand roamed down her back to cup her bottom and urge her closer while he continued to palm her breast with the other, using his thumb to entice her nipple into a stiff peak. He shifted his stance slightly, pushing the thigh she was riding more firmly against her while he urged the rocking of her hips with the hand on her bottom.

Sensations rippled along her nerve endings as his mouth slanted over hers, taking the kiss deeper. His tongue slid across hers in an erotic dance, making her hotter than she'd ever thought possible. His fingers traced the curve of her bottom, slipping lower to tease her moist folds as she continued to rock against him. The first tremor of release took her by surprise and she tried to pull back, but he was relentless. He swallowed her gasp of pleasure and urged her onward, pressing his thigh upward and adding more pressure. The tip of his finger circled her center, teasing her until she could take no more.

She tore her mouth from his and cried out at the shocking force of her climax. He didn't stop, but continued to rock her hips against him as the delicious tremors shook her body. Using his tongue, he trailed a burning path down her throat, along the slope of her breast and then finally the warm, moist heat of his mouth settled over her taut nipple.

He continued to make love to her breast as the tremors slowly subsided. Instead of leaving her sated and content, her body craved more of his touch, more intimacy. She wanted to give herself to him completely, to let him love her as he would and take her to new and better heights.

She shoved her fingers through his hair and brought his mouth back to hers for another bone-melting kiss. Certain he wouldn't be leaving her mouth anytime soon, she reached for his belt. She wanted him naked and wasted no time with the clasp and zipper of his trousers. When she had freed him, she ended the kiss, and trailed her mouth over his chest, licking her way down his torso, tasting the salt of his skin, indulging in the scent of him and the variety of textures.

She smoothed her hands along his narrow hips and pushed his trousers and briefs off as she settled to her knees in front of him.

"Ronnie?" he asked, his voice a strained whisper as he kicked the last of his clothes away.

"Shh," she murmured, and brushed his hands away when he reached for her. "Let me tilt your world for a change."

He sucked in a sharp breath as she kissed and licked and nibbled her way from his belly button and down along the dark hair that marked the path to her ultimate goal. As she traced her tongue along the impossibly perfect length of his shaft, his hands came to rest on her shoulders. His grip tightened ever so slightly when she whorled her tongue around the tip of his penis. When she took him inside her mouth, a groan ripped from his chest.

Blake knew heaven and beyond as Ronnie brought him precariously close to the edge of pleasure so intense he didn't think his legs would hold him for much longer. She took him deeply, and he shuddered, then moaned with each divine stroke of her mouth, lips and tongue. She continued to tease him toward the edge, then skillfully pulled back before he could take that final fall into oblivion. He didn't think it was possible to be any harder, but with every touch, the pressure built until he was sure he was going to explode.

Unable to bear another moment of her exquisite brand of torture, he tried to pull her away, but she refused. Her hands gripped his backside as she held him to her and continued to make love to him in ways that put his fantasies to shame. His ears buzzed. His legs started to shake. He struggled to hold back, but she ruthlessly pushed him closer to the edge until finally, he fell over the side, calling her name as he came in a hot rush. Her hands massaged his buttocks while her mouth milked him, sending him into a tailspin of pleasure so incredibly blissful he never wanted it to end.

Cognizance returned at a leisurely pace in the form of the rhythmic glide of her hands on his penis, accompanied by teasing flicks of her tongue over the tip. The world took its sweet time in righting itself, not that he was complaining.

As much as he was enjoying her attempt to keep him hard, he needed to gather his strength. She had nothing to fear in that regard, however. The night wasn't over by a long shot. He smoothed his hand over her still-damp hair and urged her to stand. She did so with agonizing slowness, gliding her hands up his torso until she slid them over his shoulders to loop them around his neck. He could've sworn her lips never left his body as she nibbled and tasted her way upward, stopping to flick her tongue across his nipple before urging his mouth down to hers for a sizzling, openmouthed kiss.

"Let's get horizontal," she said, when she ended the kiss.

He had a better idea. "Let's go for a swim."

She made a sexy little sound of protest, but didn't argue when he pulled her arms from around his neck. He left her for as long as it took to secure a condom then led her into the pool. "Do you know how to float?"

Ronnie looked up at Blake as if he'd suddenly lost

his mind. "That's not exactly what I meant by horizontal," she teased.

"Trust me," he said with a grin so wicked, it started her pulse hammering again.

"There are three things in life you're never supposed to believe," she said as they reached the center of the pool. The water barely reached his chest while she had already resorted to walking on tiptoes to keep the water below her chin.

"And they are?"

"The check is in the mail, never trust a man that says 'trust me,' and never believe a guy when he promises he won't...well, never mind the third one. We've already passed that stage."

He reached for her and drew her close. The teasing light in his gaze made her smile and had her heart melting. "If I recall, you never gave me a chance to even say that I wouldn't come in your mouth."

She slipped her arms around his neck, then wrapped her legs around his waist. "Hmm, well, I guess I can't fault you for that one."

She wiggled against him, amazed at how liberated she felt. She'd worried making love to Blake would be another mistake in her life, but with a clarity that surprised her, she suddenly understood the difference between her past mistakes and the present. Blake wasn't asking the impossible of her. He hadn't lied to her about why he wanted her. No, Blake was more honest in that he simply wanted to make love to her because he desired her. There was no ulterior motive involved, only mutual satisfaction. The choices she'd made in the past were in the past. She knew that now. Making love to Blake, agreeing to accept the beauty of their sexual exploration as nothing more than two people sharing their bodies intimately had nothing to do with repeating the past. So long as she kept her heart out of the equation, she had nothing to fear.

He hefted her higher so her thighs rested on his forearms. She locked her ankles behind his back while his hands supported her derriere. Gently massaging, his fingers moved with agonizing slowness toward her center, teasing her again as he did before. Unlike their first fiery union fueled by forty-eight hours of sexual innuendo and mental foreplay, the heat this time unfurled more leisurely in her belly, spreading outward with warm liquid pleasure and settling where she craved his touch the most. She wiggled her bottom, opening herself more in an invitation for his deliciously teasing fingers.

"You make me so hot," she whispered. "I want you inside me."

The humor faded from his gaze, and his silver eyes darkened, reminding her of thunderclouds gathering on a hot, summer Georgia afternoon after a day of blistering humidity. Like waiting for the first strike of lightning, when everything fills with anticipation, the look in his eyes sizzled with electricity, promising a storm of a different kind. A sensual storm of hunger, of desire and pure pleasure, and ten times more forceful.

Using both of his hands, he opened her folds and tenderly stroked her most sensitive place with the tip of his finger. "How hot?" he asked, applying the slightest amount of pressure.

She slid her hands into his hair and struggled for her next breath. His intimate touch, the warm water lapping her skin, and the heat in his eyes were too much. The only answer she could manage was a moan of pleasure.

"How hot, sweetheart?" He continued to stroke her while he eased two of his fingers inside her, just barely, then retreated. "What makes this," he asked, applying more pressure to her cleft, "swell and pulse for me?"

She responded to his question with a soft, keening cry of need.

"Tell me," he demanded in a voice so soft, so tender, her heart ached.

An answer hovered on her tongue, but the words frightened her. They were the wrong words. She was merely reacting to the heightened sensuality because there was no way he'd somehow managed to break past the barriers she'd erected to where she lay as easy prey, emotionally exposed and raw. Her body was in a state of sexual chaos, confusing her mind, that was all. "Because I...I want you," she said at last.

"I want you, too, sweetheart," he said. "I want you every way I can have you."

Alarm bells sounded off in her brain, parting the sensual fog as if flung into oblivion by a chilling, northerly breeze. She carefully searched his face. Passion and tenderness filled his gaze. The passion she welcomed. The tenderness made her wary. "For the moment," she clarified. Hopefully.

The corner of his mouth lifted into the semblance of a smile. "For the moment," he said as he stroked her more deeply.

He said the words she wanted to hear, but she couldn't shake the uneasy feeling he was merely placating her. *Absurd!* she thought. More than absurd. How about downright ridiculous, not to mention delusional? There was a logical explanation. It existed in the form of her long dormant hormones reawakened with a bang. Body chemistry in overload, endorphins shot into her brain to spark this bizarre form of paranoia. There was definitely *not* anything more at stake here than the taking and giving of pleasure.

"So," he said, his mouth shifting into that wicked grin she was beginning to really love seeing on his handsomely chiseled face. "You never did tell me if you could float."

10

RONNIE LIFTED ONE EYEBROW and gave Blake a skeptical look. "Floating? *On* the water?" Even in her wildest fantasies, she was having difficulty imagining making love the way he wanted. It was utterly impossible, wasn't it?

That all-too-sexy and knowing grin deepened, and didn't go a long way toward reassurance. "Lie back in the water," he instructed. "Just let your body relax."

"But...how do we..."

"I'll support you," he said, before his lips brushed over hers. He stroked her more deeply. "Trust me."

He made it difficult not to give in to his sensual demand when he had her body zinging with pleasure. Especially if he was promising more of the same. With her thighs still resting on his forearms, she followed his instructions and carefully lay back in the water. True to his word, he moved his hands to support her, holding her steady at the base of her spine. She kept her neck crooked so she could see him, using her hands to gently tread water for additional support.

"Let your head fall back in the water and just allow your arms to float on the water."

Once again she cast him a look she dearly hoped translated to, "Are you nuts?"

He chuckled. "Relax, Ronnie. You're going to enjoy this, I swear you will."

Nothing ventured, nothing gained, she supposed. And he sure seemed hell-bent on an aquatic adventure. After a deep breath, which she let out in a slow stream, she relaxed her neck and let her arms float where they wanted. He carefully eased her closer so that the back of her thighs were resting against his strong, corded biceps. Her legs opened more widely, exposing the most intimate part of her.

The contrasts were amazingly erotic. The coolness of the water lapped against her sensitized skin, while the sultry warmth of the air brushed her most intimate place. She could hear nothing but the sound of her own breathing. Above her lay a moonlit sky. The feel of Blake's hands on her body was the only reminder she was not alone in the sensual vacuum.

He gently maneuvered her, lifting her bottom slightly out of the water. Cool liquid teased her heated core and she sighed at the unexpected pleasure of contradicting sensations. Surprisingly, she found the sound of her own soft moan highly sensual.

She nearly came out of her skin at the first silky glide of his tongue on the inside of her thigh. He tasted her skin, kissed her, nipped lovingly at her flesh, giving equal attention to both thighs while alternately blowing a gentle stream of his warm breath against her exposed center. The erotic teasing had her body strung tight instantly. Desire pooled in her belly and tugged. Her need to have him taste her climbed to incredible heights.

He took his sweet time, drawing out the anticipation with each lick, nibble and kiss he placed on her body. He nibbled at the spot just above her folds, then laved his tongue over the area, coming dangerously close to her cleft. Her moans of frustration grew louder and more needy. She felt the rumble of his chuckle and the vibration of his voice as he spoke. Although the words were unintelligible, it only added to her heightened state of awareness.

Somewhere in the back of her mind, she realized that in this position, she was completely and wholly dependent on him for her pleasure. Her hands were useless to guide him, as she needed them to help her remain above the surface of the water. Since he held her in such a unique position, she'd be hard-pressed to thrust her hips in silent demand without going under. All she had was her voice, and she wasn't afraid to use it to get what she wanted.

"Blake. Please." The softly spoken plea resembled more of a shouted demand in her silent world.

Instead of complying, he lowered her bottom into the water just enough to cover her. Then with agonizing slowness, he lifted her back up again. The feel of cool water and warm air had her issuing another plea for fulfillment.

After another erotically agonizing dip in the water, his lips pressed against her. She breathed in a rush of air, and let it out in a deep moan of intense pleasure when his tongue teased and circled her opening. He made love to her with his mouth, tasting her deeply only to retreat and lave her cleft, each time applying a little more pressure, pushing her closer to the edge.

She forgot about staying afloat and just let the sensations rule her body. The water, his mouth, the intense building of pressure inside her, coiling tighter and tighter overwhelmed her senses. Her release came hard and fast when he suckled her swollen cleft, drowning her in pleasure and sizzling light. He supported her with his strong hands when she arched her back in an attempt to cull more of the electrifying shockwaves rolling through her body. Her cries were deafening, and as loud in her own ears as the frantic beating of her heart.

Before the shockwaves could subside, he moved his hands farther up her back and eased her out of the water so her legs wrapped around his waist again. The tremors continued to pulse through her as he thrust deeply inside her. She arched against him and cried out as an even more intense orgasm rocketed through her. He held her hips, guiding her up and down his shaft as he thrust into her over and over, pushing her to the edge and carrying her off the cliff into a place so emotional and sensual, she nearly wept from the beauty of it all as she came a second time.

Her body pulsed around him and she held on, unwilling to forgo a single ounce of the passion they created. The knot in her tummy tightened again and she sobbed his name in mindless wonder when another wave of ecstasy ripped through her body. He thrust one last time before she felt his body stiffen and a deep growl of pleasure tore from his throat. She felt the pulsing heat from the force of his orgasm and rode him until his body started to tremble with the aftershocks.

She clung to him and rested her head against his broad shoulder, waiting for the sensual storm to subside. As their heartbeats and breathing slowed, she was overcome by the overflowing fullness in her heart. Emotions she was too afraid to analyze and catalog for fear of discovering she'd let her guard down swamped her. The tenderness she was feeling was nothing more than the glorious afterglow of great sex. She wasn't one of those desperate females that equated the orgasm to end all orgasms with love. Great sex was...great sex. Period. End of story.

She'd once accused Blake of being a terrible liar. She should join the club because she sure wasn't much better, not when she couldn't even hope to believe a word of her own arguments.

BLAKE LEANED against the doorjamb of the elegant bathroom, entranced by the sight of Ronnie leaning over the sink to get a closer look at herself in the mirror as she applied a coat of mascara to her long, sooty lashes. The thick fluffy towel knotted at her breasts inched upward, giving him a teasing view of the curve of her backside. Heat stirred his groin. "We're going to be late if you don't get a move on, sweetheart."

She turned to look at him, mascara brush in midair. A smile full of sass canted her sinful mouth. "That wouldn't have been an issue if you hadn't joined me in the shower."

He chuckled. "I didn't hear you complaining when I washed your back."

She returned to her task. "Among other things."

"Now see, that's where we got into trouble."

She laughed, the sound light and carefree. He adored this playful side of her. Hell, there wasn't much about her he didn't find adorable, even before she'd finally let her guard down. Their relationship was no longer strictly professional, and he didn't think they could get much more personal than they had last night and this morning.

What he planned to do about it though remained a mystery, and depended a lot on Ronnie. Once Operation: Honeymoon concluded, he honestly didn't know if he could let her walk away. Whether or not forever was in the forecast, he couldn't say. But for the first time since his last disastrous relationship, which ended in a broken engagement, he wasn't about to discount the possibility of something long-term.

She twisted the cap onto the tube of mascara and looked his way again. The gold flecks in her eyes glowed, reminding him of how they'd looked when he was deep inside her.

"Instead of standing there watching me," she said, "you could check the video camera or something."

He let out a sigh and crossed his arms over his chest. "What I need to do is call Luke. He should've had something for us on Clark by now."

She outlined her lips with a thin line of deep mauve, then reached for a tube of lipstick. "You will be going outside the resort to make the call, right?"

"Yeah," he said slowly, mesmerized as she applied a coat of lipstick to her bottom lip. His state of semi-arousal blossomed into a full-blown hard-on as images of her sultry mouth and the way she'd loved him slammed into him.

She did that thing women do with their lips, then ran her tongue over her bottom lip. God, what a turn-on.

"We should let McCall or Anderson know we're boarding Clark's yacht. If you're going to call your partner, can you let one of them know? I'll be ready by the time you get back."

Making himself scarce was probably the smartest thing he could do; otherwise they might never leave their room. If applying makeup was this erotic, watching her blow-dry her hair would kill him for sure. "I have no idea what Anderson looks like or even where to find him."

She grinned and pulled off the towel she'd had wrapped around her hair. "Anderson is a her and assigned to housekeeping," she said, combing her fingers through the wet strands. "Since she hasn't come by the room yet, it could be her day off. It'd be easier if you just contacted Scott. He'll either be working the Sunset Bar or the lounge inside the main building."

With his gaze locked on hers, he pushed himself off the doorjamb and walked toward her. A hint of desire had her eyes flaring and her lips parting. He'd give just about anything to shut out the rest of the world to spend the day making love to her and learning every nuance of her personality. There wasn't much about her body he didn't know, or want to reexplore again and again.

He slid his hand along her jaw and cupped the back of her head in his palm. "You're going to have to reapply your lipstick."

She moved closer and tipped her head to look at him. "It's only lipstick."

He brought his mouth down to hers and traced her lower lip with his tongue. She made a sexy little sound in the back of her throat as her lashes fluttered closed. She arched toward him and rubbed her delectable body against his, nearly driving him to his knees. What was it about this woman that made him want to lose control?

He deepened the kiss and smoothed his hand down to cup her bottom beneath the towel. She purred and pressed against his hand. The temptation to make love to her again was agonizing.

Using every ounce of willpower he possessed, he pulled away before they went too far. He looked down at her, into her brilliant turquoise gaze, and drew the back of his hand down her silky smooth cheek. "We should talk," he said. About the future, he nearly added, but from the way her body stiffened, he kept the thought to himself...for now. "When we have more time."

"Tonight." She turned to face the mirror and started combing her hair.

He watched her reflection for a moment, but she never once looked in his direction. The ease with which they'd communicated disappeared as if it never existed. "Ronnie?" He wasn't sure what he planned to say, but the sudden change in her attitude had him worried.

She plugged her blow-dryer into the electrical outlet. "You should go. We don't have much time," she said, then dismissed him by flipping the switch on the dryer.

"HEY, BUDDY, can you tell me where a guy could get a pack of cigarettes around here?"

Blake impatiently tapped his fingers on the smooth wood surface of the bar in the resort's main lounge. McCall and another bartender were on duty, and Blake made sure the other bartender heard his question.

McCall set a pair of drinks in front of a young couple before turning his attention to Blake. "Sorry, pal. No smoking." He hitched his thumb toward a sign discreetly posted behind the bar. "State law."

"Yeah, I figured as much. I can't even find a cigarette machine around this place." He had no interest in purchasing cigarettes, but he did need a minute alone with McCall.

"There's a convenience store about a block away," McCall said. "Right next to an outdoor café and coffeehouse." He checked his watch. "It'll take you about five minutes to get there."

Blake thanked him for the directions then headed toward the coffeehouse. He figured he had about ten minutes before McCall joined him, so he made use of the time by locating a telephone booth near his destination to place a call to Luke. He dialed Luke's cell phone number. His partner picked up on the second ring.

"Stone."

Blake didn't waste time with preliminaries. "Anything on Clark?"

"Ah, Blake old buddy," Luke said in that way of his that reminded Blake of someone who hadn't a care in the world. "How's the honeymoon?"

A lot more real than he ever intended, not that he'd be sharing that bit of information with his partner. "Not bad as far as honeymoons go. Find anything for me?"

The sounds of L.A. traffic buzzed in the background. "Only about fifty kilos of synthetic blow."

Blake let out a low whistle. "No shit. How'd you stumble onto that?"

"Well, now that's the real interesting part. A dear sweet old woman is helping her daughter run a fabric store over on Cahuenga Boulevard and is living in an apartment upstairs. She heard strange noises coming from the alley and called L.A.'s finest. Dispatch sent a black-and-white to check it out and you'll never guess what they found."

"A drug distribution center," Blake answered. "Did you find a connection to Clark and the building?"

"Yeah. We have a connection," Luke said. The laughter left his voice. "But nothing to tie him directly to it, as usual."

Blake listened as Luke explained that the location where they found the coke was leased to a Rhonda

Hillman, who just happened to be the sister-in-law of Billy Hillman.

"Who the hell is Billy Hillman?" Blake asked.

"Small-timer until recently. I suspect nepotism."

Blake swore as he saw Scott McCall turn the corner. "Luke. Get to the point."

"Billy Hillman is Cheryl Hillman's little brother. Or should I say Cheryl Hillman *Clark's* little brother. We've got an APB out on him and should have him picked up before the end of the day. When they get him, I'll personally see what the guy has to say."

Dammit! While he and Ronnie had taken their undercover operation under the covers, Clark had moved a shipment. There'd been nothing on the surveillance tape other than the pair of exhibitionists. Either the drugs weren't being siphoned through the resort, or they'd been picked up elsewhere and taken right from Clark's yacht to the harbor. Or, the drugs never came off the yacht, but directly from the resort, which didn't explain Clark's presence. It didn't make sense. At least not yet.

The background noise disappeared suddenly, indicating Luke had either gone inside or was sitting in his vehicle.

"Don't you just love life's little coincidences?"

As far as Blake was concerned, Clark's arrival at Seaport and the seizure of fifty kilos of cocaine was no coincidence. "So what are you doing there? I thought you were still on the uptown robberies."

"Just a short break. Watch Commander turned the call over to Vice, and Forbes sent me to check it out.

Thought it might be related to what you're doing. How much longer you got out there, buddy?"

"Clark arrived last night and Agent Carmichael managed to get us an invite onto his yacht. We'll be on board within the hour. If we find anything, we could wrap this up in the next day or so."

"You're not going to find anything, Blake. I guarantee it. Whatever might have been on board that yacht is being cataloged as we speak. What you need to find out is why Clark is showing up every ten days."

"I've got to run."

"Watch your back, buddy," Luke said in a sobering tone. "The boys aren't just cataloging coke. We're calling ATF for this one."

If the LAPD was bringing Alcohol, Tobacco and Firearms into this, then the case was bigger than any of them suspected. "I'll be in touch," Blake said. He hung up the phone and signaled to McCall.

"Problem?" McCall asked, once they were seated at an outdoor table of the coffeehouse.

Blake shoved his hand through his hair and leaned back in the plastic patio chair. "We have a connection to Clark and the coke," he said, then let McCall in on the information he'd received from Luke. "I don't think the coke's being moved on Clark's yacht. I think it's being manufactured somewhere at Seaport."

"No way. We've found nothing to even indicate there's a lab at the resort, or the island for that matter."

"The reason Ronnie and I are here is because you and Anderson have no access to the resort."

"Anderson has seen more of this place than I have. Believe me, she's looked."

"It's there, McCall. I can feel it."

"I'll talk to Anderson," he said. "So what's up? I've got ten minutes."

Blake quickly explained how they'd received an invitation to join Clark aboard the *Mary Alice*. "We're hoping to find some kind of evidence, but after talking to Luke, I'm having my doubts."

"Take advantage of the opportunity for a look around. You could get lucky." McCall smiled suddenly. "Speaking of lucky, you and Carmichael having a good time?"

Blake felt the same twisting in his gut he felt the last time he'd met with McCall. This time however, he recognized the accompanying emotion as jealousy. "She's my partner," he said coldly.

McCall shrugged his quarterback-wide shoulders. "Wouldn't be the first time."

Blake pulled off his sunglasses and gave the agent a sharp stare. "Why don't you just say what's on your mind, McCall."

"Carmichael's got a rep for engaging in extracurricular activity on the job, that's all. She's a looker. If I were in your place, I'd have to wonder if maybe..."

The urge to slam his fist into McCall's smug face was strong enough to have Blake clenching and unclenching his hands. Not a good sign. "And you feel compelled to share this with me to enhance public relations between our departments, is that it?" Blake asked sarcastically. "Look, Ronnie's past is hers. It's none of my business."

McCall leaned forward and braced his arms on the plastic tabletop. "You should make it your business, Hammond. Her partners have a tendency of ending up in body bags."

I was cleared and you know it.

Her sharply spoken words to McCall came back to him. He'd suspected there was something more to the tension between Ronnie and the other agent, but she'd evaded his question, simply stating that she'd had an affair that ended badly. He should let the subject drop. It really was none of his business, but his own past experience made him wary. "Meaning?" he prompted, knowing he should go to Ronnie with his questions. To only have her evade him again?

McCall waved away the waitress before she could approach their table. "The first time, she wasn't at fault. She was a rookie with a veteran hard-ass for a partner. Pete Johnson liked to do things his way. Her old man could've pulled a few strings and had her moved to anybody else in the department, let her get some experience before throwing her out on the street, but old Carmichael's a tough SOB and I guess he wanted his daughter to take after him.

"They were on a stakeout in Oak Glen that turned ugly, and Johnson was killed. Carmichael was too green and put in a bad situation without any backup. She was damned lucky to get out alive. Could've happened to any one of us."

Blake agreed. No matter how careful, how methodically planned, an undercover assignment could go wrong in the flash of an instant. There were too many variables for anything on the street to be a sure thing.

"She did take two or three of the bastards out, though," McCall continued. "Shook her up pretty bad, too. It's rough the first time."

"It's always tough when you have no other choice but to draw your weapon," Blake said. The psychological aspects could be the end of a career in law enforcement, and was one of the reasons psych clearance was required before returning to full duty. "And the second time?"

"To be fair to Carmichael," McCall said, "no one really knows exactly what happened out there. Rumor and fact have a way of getting mixed up until the truth is blown out of proportion. It doesn't take much for rumor to become fact, you know what I mean? It didn't help either that she won't defend herself to any of us, so we believe what we believe."

"She says she was cleared," Blake pointed out.

McCall leaned back in the chair. "I only know what I know. Like I said, she never talked about it except to IA and the shrinks. But you wonder, you know? How much of the rumors are true? Hard to tell sometimes. I mean, how well do you really know a person?"

As much as Blake wanted to argue otherwise on Ronnie's behalf, he couldn't. She'd stoically kept her past to herself, even when he'd questioned her about it. Oh, he knew her body, her touch, the way her eyes changed color when she was aroused or angry or teasing. He knew the scent of her perfume, and the way her rich sable hair glistened in the moonlight. None of what he knew really amounted to anything other than confirming his attraction to her. "You fire your weapon and IA investigates," he finally said by paltry way of defense.

"True. But they really stir up a lot of shit when one agent takes down another."

"What are you saying?" he asked carefully. "That she shot her partner?"

McCall nodded. "Right between the eyes."

11

BLAKE SAT next to Ronnie on the small motorboat heading toward Alister Clark's yacht, his mind still reeling from his conversation with Scott McCall. He felt as though he'd been tied to two horses running in opposite directions. The part that had fallen for Ronnie was being pulled in one direction and sympathized with her, wanted to shield her and protect her from the ugliness and speculation that had followed her during her entire career with the DEA. The part of him that was all cop, carried a ton of suspicion and doubt, and was being pulled by the stronger horse.

There wasn't a cop on the force who'd accept a partner with the kind of rumors surrounding Ronnie without one hell of a fight. Himself included. If he'd known about her past record, he could honestly say he would have moved heaven and earth to not be a part of Operation: Honeymoon regardless of the sparks of attraction that had been growing between them from that first meeting. He'd already had an experience with a bad cop, and he didn't want another.

There was only one way to get to the truth, and that was to confront her with the information. He still had doubts about her willingness to be honest with him, especially considering how she'd evaded his questions on the subject once already. His only hope would be laying it all on the line, everything, including his feelings for her, which were as still new and as confusing as the tale McCall shared with him.

After all she'd been through, Blake understood her need to protect herself emotionally. Maybe if she knew how he really felt, that he saw their relationship as more than just a temporary partnership but something deeper and lasting, and if he admitted he knew about the rumors surrounding the deaths of two of her partners, then she'd feel compelled to tell him the truth. The only thing he did know for certain, was that if she wasn't willing to be honest with him, then there would be no future for them. A relationship was nothing without trust and honesty, and if she wasn't willing to give those to him without question, then as hard as it would be to let her slip out of his life, he would say goodbye once they wrapped up the case.

They'd been greeted by a middle-aged man who'd introduced himself as Nick. With his slightly graying hair, kind brown eyes and a bit of a paunch, the guy looked about as criminally connected as a guy in a Norman Rockwell painting.

Ronnie glanced in Blake's direction and smiled, her turquoise eyes filled with affection. The signs of her apprehension before he'd left to meet with McCall were nonexistent, and he wondered about the change.

She lifted her hand to shield her eyes from the bright glare of the sun reflecting off the water and pointed toward the bow. "Is that it?" she called out to

Nick, indicating a spectacular ninety footer anchored at the mouth of a cove.

Nick slowed the motorboat as they neared the yacht. "That'd be her, Mrs. St. Claire."

"Isn't it beautiful, Blake?" she exclaimed. "You could sail around the world on something that large."

"Perhaps we should consider one of our own," he said for Nick's benefit. "I'll ask Alister to give us a tour once we board, then we can decide."

Her hand settled on his thigh and she squeezed gently. "How you spoil me, Blake."

"Don't get too excited. We haven't even had a chance to look around yet."

She squeezed his thigh again until he looked at her. "You're asking the impossible," she said with a laugh. The expression in her eyes changed and she gave him a steady look. "I'm already wired for sound."

Nick chuckled, but Blake ignored it. He pushed his sunglasses down and stared at her in stunned surprise as her meaning became crystal clear. She gave him a slight nod, and he bit back the string of swear words hovering on his tongue. She'd taken an enormous risk that could have them both taking a permanent nap on a metal slab with tags wrapped around their big toes. They never discussed wearing a wire, and if they had, it sure as hell wouldn't have been her.

She bit her lip and looked away as Nick brought the motorboat alongside the *Mary Alice*.

Nick killed the engine. "Prepare to board," he said, then waited until the transport was secure before assisting Ronnie aboard the yacht. Blake followed close behind her with Nick bringing up the rear.

"Right this way." Nick led them to the foredeck beneath the shade of a cabana, then politely disappeared. A crew member dressed in formal black tie appeared at Ronnie's side and asked what she'd like to drink.

Blake knew Clark had money, and a lot of it, but he was still surprised by the wealth the bastard had amassed over the last ten years. Not all of Clark's business ventures were the kind that would land him behind bars for a very long time, but Blake still doubted his legitimate business holdings kept him in his current lifestyle. In his opinion, that made Alister Clark twice as dangerous as the average thug.

Ronnie surveyed the small crowd. "I don't see him."

A variety of guests in conversation milled about the deck while two other crewmen, also dressed in formal attire, carried silver serving trays filled with hors d'oeuvres. Their waiter returned within seconds with a glass of white wine and an imported beer.

Blake thanked him for their drinks. "Where's your employer?" he asked before the waiter could slip away.

"I believe Mr. Clark is in a brief meeting belowdeck, sir. Please, do make yourself comfortable. He should be joining his guests again shortly."

Once the waiter was out of earshot, Ronnie lifted her glass to her lips. "So what do we do now?" she whispered.

He took her by the elbow and steered her port side. "We look like we're having an intimate conversation while enjoying the view."

Ronnie peered over the railing. He moved behind her and trapped her between his body and the rail. Pressed against her back, he expected to feel the recording device, but all he felt were her soft, gentle curves. If any of the guests happened to be paying attention, they'd see nothing but a couple of honeymooners sharing a personal moment.

Using the tip of his beer bottle, he pointed over the side to nothing in particular. "What the hell do you think you're doing?" he said in her ear.

"Trying to look interested in the water you're pointing out," she sassed, then indicated toward the rear of the ship.

"Where's the wire?" he asked. She wore a sleeveless tropical-print dress that fell to midcalf, and a pair of sandals. The material didn't cling, but it did outline her figure to perfection.

"Where no one will find it," she said quietly.

"Are you *trying* to get us killed?" he hissed in a harsh whisper. "And why the hell didn't you discuss it with me first?"

She turned and looped her arm around his neck and urged his head down. "There wasn't time," she said against his ear. "I made the decision and went for it."

"Exactly who is monitoring you?"

"No one. The recording equipment is in the room."

"This is not a good idea," he told her. "I've got a bad feeling about this."

"There's nothing to worry about. And if something should go wrong, at least when our people secure our room they'll have it on tape. Besides, someone would have to get *very* close and personal to know I'm wired."

He struggled not to allow the alignment of her body with his to distract him, but it was close to impossible. Where Ronnie was concerned, he was the one who was wired, to every curve, every nuance, everything...except her version of the truth regarding her past.

He wrapped his arm around her waist and pulled her closer against him. "Provided you're not out of range. Keep your eyes open and watch your back," he said. "There was a large bust in L.A. early this morning, and Luke found a connection to Clark. I'm betting this 'meeting' that has our host occupied is related."

"If he's already moved the cargo then what are we doing here?" She muttered a whispered curse and pulled away. "Alister, how good to see you again," she said, pasting an overly bright smile on her face.

Blake moved to Ronnie's side and kept his arm around her waist as Clark, a woman Blake guessed to be Clark's wife, Cheryl, and another couple joined them at the railing.

Clark shook hands with Blake. "Nick told me you were aboard. I apologize for keeping you waiting. A problem with one of my investments. I'm sure you understand, Blake."

"Indeed I do," Blake said. More than Clark imagined. If Luke was right, then Clark's "investment" problems were just beginning. "Ronnie and I were admiring the view."

"Yes, it is spectacular. Sunset is particularly stunning, isn't it, my dear?" He turned his attention to the statuesque redhead at his side, who offered a bland smile that didn't reach her crystal-clear, blue eyes. "My wife, Cheryl," Clark said by way of introduction. "She's not fond of sailing."

Cheryl swept them with her bored gaze, then promptly excused herself. She lifted a flute of champagne from a passing waiter, and pulled the sarong shirt from her waist before positioning herself on a deck chair beneath the warmth of the sun.

Clark turned to the dark-haired man beside him. "This is a friend and business associate of mine, Steven Ramsey, and his friend, Hilary Jacobs. Blake and Veronica St. Claire. From Savannah, right?"

"Yes. And it's Ronnie," she said, and flashed them one of her high-wattage smiles. She added something polite that Blake tuned out as his mind quickly spun. He'd seen Ramsey somewhere before, but for the life of him, he couldn't place exactly where. The chances of Ramsey being a collar hardly seemed likely. The man was too polished, too smooth and, by all appearances, well-bred. This was not the kind of guy they picked up on a corner dealing crack to the local criminal element, or even a minor supplier.

From his cursory glance at the guests aboard the *Mary Alice*, he would be hard-pressed to pick any one of them out of a lineup as the type to be associated with the illegal drug trade. Of course that didn't mean they were clean, but more than likely, underground business associates, who would not be found on the list of invited guests to any social affair hosted by Alister Clark.

Ramsey spoke to Ronnie in greeting then extended his hand to Blake. Blake shook the proffered hand and waited for some sign of recognition from Ramsey. He wasn't disappointed.

"Have we met somewhere?" Ramsey asked him, his dark brown eyes watchful. "You look familiar to me."

Blake ignored Ronnie's sharp glance in his direction. He snagged her hand and gave her what he hoped was a silent command to let him do the talking.

"Do you get to Savannah often?" Blake countered. Damn. He hadn't been lying when he told Ronnie he had a bad feeling. He just hadn't expected it to be in the form of recognition by one of Clark's other guests.

Ramsey shook his head, but remained watchful. "Can't say that I've ever had the pleasure."

Hilary, a petite blonde with a pert nose and intelligent hazel eyes smiled up at Ramsey. She couldn't have been more than twenty-two, and at least a good twenty years Ramsey's junior. "What kind of business are you in, Mr. St. Claire?" she asked, turning her attention to Blake.

"Blake's involved in a little of just about everything," Ronnie answered. "Nothing holds his attention for too long."

"Alister tells us you're on your honeymoon." A wistful note entered Hilary's voice as she cast a quick but meaningful glance in Ramsey's direction. "I would think a party would be the last place you'd want to be."

Ronnie laughed and smiled at Hilary. She couldn't say she was overly fond of Clark's snooty wife, but Hilary at least appeared to be a little more genuine, even if the chances were high that there was a Mrs. Ramsey somewhere in the background who turned a blind eye to her husband's extramarital affairs. "I couldn't resist Alister's invitation to go sailing. Now if I can just convince him to give me a tour of this wonderful boat." She leaned toward the younger woman and added in a bad stage whisper, "We're thinking of buying one for ourselves."

Clark slipped his hand into the pocket of his neatly pressed navy slacks. "I'm afraid there's been a change in plans and we won't be able to take her out as I'd hoped. We're pulling anchor tonight."

"Allow me to show you around then," Hilary said, reaching for Ronnie's hand and pulling her away from Blake's side before she could protest. To the men she said, "You go ahead and talk all the business you want. Us girls will be just fine. The staterooms are simply gorgeous."

"I don't—"

"Don't worry," Hilary said sweetly, cutting off Blake's objection. "I promise to bring your bride back to you very soon."

Ronnie gave Blake a helpless shrug and allowed herself to be led away by Hilary toward the rear of the ship. She hadn't planned on being separated from

Blake, nor leaving him alone with Clark, but she couldn't very well refuse Hilary's invitation without drawing suspicion after her request for a tour. Not to mention how much Ramsey's comment had her worried. She had no idea if Blake might know the other man, but the fact that he'd recognized Blake was enough to have her anxious to get them both the hell off the yacht.

"Wait until you see the staterooms, Ronnie," Hilary said again, as they descended the companionway. "Alister not only had the interior decorated by one of L.A.'s top designers, but he also made sure his guests would have every convenience imaginable."

Ronnie feigned excitement, although on some level, she admittedly couldn't help but be impressed by the elegance of the main cabin with its plush carpet, rich mahogany furnishings and exquisite fabrics. "Have you and Steven known Alister long?"

Hilary guided Ronnie down the alleyway to the first stateroom on their tour. "I haven't, but Steven has for quite some time. I think they met while he was still practicing law."

Ronnie peered into the room and made the appropriate appreciative sounds before asking, "Steven's an attorney?" The room was immaculate, and obviously unused.

"He was until he became a judge a few years ago. The rest of the rooms are occupied and pretty much like this one, but I don't think Alister or Cheryl would mind if I showed you their stateroom. It's incredible."

A chill ran down Ronnie's spine as she followed

Hilary farther down the alleyway. It was entirely possible Blake had testified before Ramsey in a criminal trial. She and Blake had to find a plausible excuse to return to shore because she was dead certain it'd only be a matter of time before Ramsey recalled exactly where he'd seen Blake. And if Ramsey and Clark were friends, it'd be an easy bet the Honorable Steven Ramsey was on the take and would be sure to share Blake's identity with his partner in crime.

Hilary opened the door to Clark's stateroom. "Here we are... Ronnie, are you ill?" Concern filled the younger woman's innocent gaze. "You look positively pale."

No, not ill, afraid, dammit. Terrified that Ramsey would remember where he'd seen Blake and their cover would be blown. If Clark discovered the truth while they were still aboard the *Mary Alice*, they'd end up as shark bait.

Ronnie had never fainted a day in her life, nor was she particularly squeamish, but if pretending otherwise had Hilary running to bring Blake to her side, then so be it. With one hand on her stomach and the other on her forehead, she stumbled into Clark's stateroom. "I need to lie down," she said in a pathetically weak voice, and aimed straight for the large bed across the room.

Hilary darted into the head and came back with a cool cloth which she promptly laid over Ronnie's forehead.

"It must be something I ate," Ronnie lied.

Hilary sat on the edge of the bed beside her, genuine concern etched on her face. What the woman was doing mixed up with someone like Clark and Ramsey, Ronnie could only guess. She supposed any young, naive girl wanting a better life for herself, was attracted to wealth and power, no matter which side of the law she found it. "Maybe the sea doesn't agree with you. Can I get you something?"

Ronnie offered up a thin smile, and what she hoped was a helpless expression. "Would you mind finding Blake for me?"

Hilary bit her lip as if weighing the decision to leave her alone in Clark's stateroom. Finally, she stood and walked to the door.

"Hilary?" Ronnie called out as Hilary passed through the door and into the alleyway. "Could you close the door? I wouldn't want anyone to see me like this."

Hilary gave her one last look filled with concern before closing the door. Ronnie hesitated all of two seconds before she was off the bed, searching drawers and closet space. Maritime law required that every captain keep a log of the ship's travels, and privately owned yachts were no exception. Not that she really expected to find evidence of illegal cargo aboard, but if she could at least get a look at the log, she and Blake might learn where Clark disappeared to during his ten-day sojourns away from the island.

Time was at a premium and she'd given a cursory inspection of every possible location inside the stateroom, except wherever Clark kept the ship's logbook. Which meant it was probably on the bridge. Truck drivers sometimes kept a second set of logbooks. In order to make a living, they often drove more than the hours allowed by law, something a second set of books allowed them to do, just so long as they didn't get caught by the DOT officials. If truck drivers did it, there was a chance Clark did, as well.

She couldn't afford the risk of assuming that Hilary would send Blake alone. Being caught with her hand in the proverbial cookie jar wouldn't go very far in ensuring their continued health. Hilary might be a sweet girl, but she was still the mistress of a possibly dirty judge.

She stood in the center of the elegant stateroom, mentally cataloging every nook, cranny and surface, discarding each as improbable hiding places or as already searched. The door to the head stood open. Unlikely, she thought, but dashed inside anyway. As quietly and quickly as possible, she opened drawers and cabinets, finding nothing besides the standard items one would find in any bathroom. She peeked inside the shower, and that's when she found it.

Obviously someone had been in a hurry because the door to a small compartment hadn't been properly closed. She listened for a second to reassure herself no one would find her snooping, then stepped into the shower and gave the hinged door a tug. Tucked inside the small wood-paneled compartment were ledgers, cash and a few items of expensive jewelry. She reached for the ledger and flipped it open. Columns of figures and notations filled the pages of the manifest, listing quantities of cargo carried on the *Mary Alice*. Illegal cargo.

She pulled another bound ledger from the compartment and found more of the same, quietly reading some of the entries aloud for the benefit of the wire. The final book she retrieved was filled with notes of various ports of call. Ports she'd wager would not be found on the logbooks kept on the bridge.

They had evidence.

Ronnie stilled at the sound of approaching voices, followed by the distinct click of the door to the stateroom being opened.

"Where is she?" There was no mistaking the threat in the cultured timbre of Alister Clark's voice, confirming that she was as good as dead if he found her.

BLAKE WAS GETTING ANTSY and having trouble following the conversation with Lloyd Barrett and Sherman Jones, a pair of high-ranking VP's from two of the state's largest banking establishments. Something to do with the Federal Reserve not lowering interest rates, he thought, as Barrett waxed on about a snowball effect. Blake's only interest was in Ronnie and returning to shore as soon as possible. Since it'd taken him less than ten minutes to place Ramsey, he knew it'd only be a matter of time before the criminal court judge returned the favor.

She'd been gone for nearly forty-five minutes. Surely she should have returned by now. The fact that Clark had disappeared, as well, only added to his anxious state of mind.

His gaze slipped to Ramsey, who was deep in conversation with an elderly gentleman Blake recognized as the head of a movie studio, thanks to a recent sex scandal that'd been plastered all over the news in recent months. Sex, drugs and rock 'n' roll. They always made headlines in L.A.

If Ramsey had placed him, so far as Blake could tell, there hadn't been a single outward sign of recognition. He could only hope the judge had all but forgotten the trial of a minor drug offender, where Blake and his former partner, Mason O'Neill, had testified. A case that had the defendant walking on a bullshit technicality.

He returned his attention to Barrett and Jones, offering a few noncommittal responses until a movement caught his attention. Hilary appeared at Ramsey's side, smiling prettily at the lecherous movie mogul. And she was alone.

Ronnie was in trouble. He didn't believe in coincidences, and there was no other explanation for Hilary's presence and Clark's disappearance while Ronnie was nowhere in sight.

He could either approach Hilary and ask her to take him to Ronnie, which might lead to a confrontation, or he could slip quietly away and go in search of her himself.

Since Hilary had mentioned showing Ronnie the staterooms, he excused himself from the two banking officials and went in search of the companionway that would take him belowdeck. After one wrong turn that had him in a small, topside galley, he located the companionway and carefully descended the narrow stairwell.

A large cabin that could easily accommodate fifty or so guests was occupied by two women deep in discussion. They were dressed conservatively, and were a good ten to fifteen years above the median feminine age group he'd seen on the yacht thus far. Too old to be mistresses, he figured them for wives.

"You look lost, sailor," commented the younger of the two. She had a welcoming smile and a hint of laughter in her voice.

"It appears I've lost my wife," he said, a bit taken aback by how natural the word felt on his tongue. "Dark hair, wearing a print dress?"

The other, older woman pointed toward a narrow hallway. "Try down there. I believe I heard one of the guests say someone had gotten seasick."

"If you don't find her, Kathryn and I will be glad to keep you company, sailor." Her throaty laughter filled the air.

Normally, he would have found her flirtatiousness comical, considering she was around his mother's age or older, but he had a more urgent matter requiring his attention. He headed off down the alleyway Kathryn indicated to the staterooms. Without bothering to knock, he tried each door only to find them unoccupied. By the time he reached the second to last door, his body was strung tightly.

He approached the final door at the end of the alleyway and stopped. The distinct sound of nervous feminine laughter drifted through the door.

Ronnie's laughter.

He flung the door open and stared in stunned disbelief. He'd been worried for her safety, his imagination firing off any number of dangerous scenarios, but he couldn't have been more wrong. Shock slowly faded, replaced by the sharp pang of something infinitely more unnerving...red-hot jealousy.

Clark sat in a chair with a drink in his hand, looking no more dangerous than the two financial blowhards topside, while his "wife" stood in the middle of Clark's elegant stateroom wearing nothing but a thick fluffy towel and a smile.

12

BLAKE SWORE VIVIDLY and started pacing the room again. Any resemblance to the cool, calm and collected cop he'd been since he started with the force evaporated the minute he found Ronnie half-naked in Clark's stateroom. His feelings had gone from surprise, to the sharp sting of irrational jealousy, and finally to a low simmering anger that she'd acted without consulting him, risking both their lives. Just what the hell was she trying to prove, or to whom, is what he wanted to know.

"Your little stunt back there could've gotten us both killed." He didn't care if his voice was rising. He was pissed.

She'd be smart to keep her mouth shut and just let him get it out of his system, but he'd have an easier time convincing the sun to rise at dusk and set at dawn.

Her delicate features were calm as she leaned back in the Queen Anne chair. "I don't know why you're blustering," she said in a reasonable tone that had him close to grinding his teeth. "We finally have enough evidence to end this case."

"You don't know? You don't know!" He shook his head and looked to the ceiling. "She doesn't know," he railed to the heavens. She didn't know that he was twisted up in knots so tight he couldn't breathe when he thought about what could've happened to her. She was clueless to the fact that just the thought of losing her made his heart ache to the point of physical pain. She had no idea he could have easily killed Clark with his bare hands if the bastard had harmed her.

He shoved his hand through his hair, wishing he could push away the raw emotions clamping his chest in a viselike grip just as easily. He couldn't, so he gave her a level stare instead. "Does the Fourth Amendment mean *anything* to you? Is probable cause even a *part* of your vocabulary?"

She let out a slow even breath, but the quick flash of fire flaring to life in her turquoise eyes indicated her patience was in danger of snapping, as well. "There's no need to be sarcastic. As soon as Clark's yacht is seized they'll find the compartment when they perform the search. The same way I found it."

Okay, so she had a valid point. The Coast Guard would seize the *Mary Alice* and have it searched, but their hands were tied until they had something more to go on than Ronnie's Fourth Amendment violation. They'd already contacted McCall, and he and Anderson were on standby waiting for word to move. He'd called Luke and brought him up to speed, but until Billy Hillman was brought in for questioning, there wasn't a damn thing they could do but wait. No judge would justify a search warrant just because some guy's brother-in-law was involved in the seizure of a mass quantity of drugs. So until Luke worked magic and not only brought Hillman in, but had him giving up the goods on Clark, Blake and Ronnie had no other choice but to wait it out.

"Okay then," he said sharply. "Fine. You're right. So why don't you tell me why the hell you were parading around naked in front of Clark."

"Not naked. I had on a towel. A bath sheet actually."

He crossed his arms over his chest. "Oh, forgive me. A bath sheet. Well, hell, you were dressed to play belle of the ball then."

The heat in her narrowed gaze intensified. "I did what I had to do so we wouldn't end up as Jaws's next main course. You know damn well I was doing my job."

"Do I? It's not like you told me what you had planned. You're a cowboy, Ronnie, and cowboys are dangerous. You're not a goddamn island," he roared. "You have a partner in case you haven't noticed."

Her hands gripped the arms of the chair. "I didn't plan to get caught searching Clark's cabin," she fired back at him. "The opportunity was there and I took it. Don't you dare stand there and tell me you wouldn't have done the same thing. By pretending to be seasick I was able to send Hilary to get you. She told me Ramsey was a judge and it was easy to put together why she thought you were familiar. I had to let you know, but instead of finding you, she brought Clark back with her while I was standing in his shower with some very interesting reading material."

She pushed out of the chair and walked toward

him. If he wasn't so angry with her for scaring the hell out of him, she just might have found all that fire and grit sexy as hell.

"I didn't have time to think, Blake. I reacted. Since they thought I was seasick, I closed the door and did a damn fine job of pretending to *be* sick. It worked because thankfully no one was quite that willing to come into the bathroom to watch a woman puking her guts out. It gave me time to stow the evidence back where I found it, turn on the shower and strip because I'd ruined my dress, which, by the way, is still soaking wet and probably ruined. And wasn't it lucky for me that Ramsey's mistress is a kindhearted person and loaned me a pair of jeans that are so damn tight they're making me cranky."

His gaze slid to the jeans in question. His body stirred as he admired how the faded denim hugged and emphasized her gently rounded hips. "What exactly happened to the wire you were wearing?" he asked, more to keep his mind on their conversation and not the way his own trousers were starting to feel just a little too snug.

A wry grin turned up the corners of her mouth as she unbuttoned the jeans and tugged the red-striped cotton top from the waistband. "I told you no one would find it unless they got way too personal," she said.

She lowered the zipper, and he couldn't quite believe what he was seeing. Sure enough, she had the credit-card-thin device taped to her skin right at her bikini line. He didn't even want to think about Clark getting anywhere close enough to Ronnie to discover the wire.

She carefully pulled off the tape and wire, muttering something about breathing when she removed the jeans next. His mouth went dry as she peeled off the snug denim, revealing nothing but smooth, bare skin. "That still doesn't explain how you ended up half-naked and alone with Clark."

She shot him a look filled with impatience, crossed the room to the dresser and tugged open a drawer. "Why are you making that one detail the issue here?" she demanded, stepping into a pair of white satin panties. "Why does it even matter?"

"It matters."

She wiggled out of the too-snug top and tossed it aside. "No," she said, reaching behind her to fasten the hook of her matching satin bra. "You answer me this time. Why is that such an issue with you?"

He closed the distance between them. "Because," he said quietly, as he smoothed the back of his hand down her cheek, "the thought of Clark anywhere near you scares the hell out of me. Do you have any idea what could've happened if he hadn't bought your excuse, or worse, found you were wearing a wire?"

She pulled back and turned away from him. Not just physically, he thought, as she walked to the closet, but emotionally, as well. He watched her pull on her own pair of jeans followed by a plain white-cotton button-down shirt, knowing the time had come to lay everything on the line. Time was short, and before long, they'd be involved in a flurry of activity and probably not have another chance to be alone.

She slid the closet door closed then turned to face him. "I was doing my job, Blake," she said, her voice all too calm and alarmingly void. "I did what I had to do, and it kept us alive."

He took a step toward her, but she turned and walked into the bathroom. He followed her. She couldn't keep running, not from him. Not if their future counted on her letting him inside where she kept her secrets, her fears and, dammit, her heart.

He crossed his arms and leaned against the doorjamb. "Were you?" he asked. "How am I supposed to know if you keep running and won't talk to me?"

She leaned over the sink, her forearms resting on the marble surface, and buried her face in her hands. The seconds ticked by, and when she didn't move, he feared he'd lost her again to wherever it was she retreated when things got tough emotionally. Finally, she lifted her head and looked over at him. "I'm not running anywhere until we bring in Clark."

"This isn't about Clark."

"Then what?"

"Tell me about your last partner."

She looked away again, straightened and turned on the tap. "Trevor and I had an affair," she said, her voice flat.

"Is that all?" he pressed, already knowing the answer, but he needed to hear the truth from her. Needed her to trust him not to turn on her like the agents she worked with, and based on comments she'd made, her own father, as well, because she'd failed to live up to some unrealistic image of supercop.

He waited patiently while she washed her hands, then her face. "You talked to Scott," she said, reaching for a hand towel. "What did he tell you?"

"Everything he knew."

She tossed the towel on the counter and turned to face him. Pain mingled with fear in her eyes, and it just about ripped his heart in two. He hated that he was doing this to her, but she had to trust him.

She walked past him into the bedroom, where she climbed to the middle of the bed and pulled her legs up to her chest, wrapping her arms around her calves. "He doesn't know half of what he thinks he does," she said, once he sat on the edge. "No one does."

"So he says."

"I shouldn't have to justify myself to them. To anyone. I did what I had to do."

Her voice caught and he nearly pulled her into his arms and told her to forget about it. Instead, he pushed her. "He said you were implicated in something pretty nasty."

She laughed, but the sound held no humor. "Oh, I was involved all right, but not like everyone believes. I can give you a list of excuses why it happened. Young. Inexperienced. Maybe even a little arrogance, too. But they're just factors that don't excuse what happened. Did Scott tell you they call me Widowmaker Carmichael?"

With sudden clarity, he realized her struggle to always be in control stemmed not from some Napoleonic impulse or even requisite DEA arrogance, but from a need to protect herself from the pain of never truly belonging to a club where she'd never wanted a membership. More importantly, she used it to shield herself from being hurt emotionally. If she never let anyone in, then no one could hurt her. At the end of the day, that kind of philosophy resulted in a lonely existence.

"Trevor Greenwood was a charmer," she said, breaking the silence. "Not to mention that I had believed he was a damned good agent...at first. After the shoot-out at Oak Glen when Pete Johnson, my first partner, was killed, Trevor was the only agent in my unit who didn't give me a hard time. To give them credit, I can't blame the guys entirely. They weren't intentionally cruel, but they like to blow off steam and a twisted sense of humor is one way to do it. I hadn't learned yet to block it out and move on like they had, and I was still sensitive about the shootings and the fact that I'd lost my partner. Trevor seemed to sense that and tried to shield me from it. It was no wonder I was relieved when they told me I was going to be his partner."

She turned her head and rested her cheek on her knees to look at him. "Trevor always seemed to have the inside track on a deal going down, as if he had this great sixth sense or something. I even wanted to be like him. Well, he had the inside track all right, but it was far from legit. His busts were never big enough to make headlines, and while he was busy busting up some rinky-dink supplier, the big ones were always just out of reach. He'd claim he'd gotten a tip, almost always anonymous, and then we'd go out, watch, wait, but nothing ever went down unless it was a minor bust."

The DEA's idea of a minor bust differed greatly from that of the vice squad. While Vice considered a local dealer selling pot or meth out of his garage small-time, DEA's version of minor was anything with a street value of less than twenty grand. "He was using decoys," he clarified.

"Exactly. Trevor knew where the real deal was going down, but he kept us away from it by offering up phony leads. The ones we did get were 'gimmes' from the drug cartel Trevor was involved in. It kept the agency happy and away from the truth, while Trevor had himself a nice stellar record of busts and a safe full of hush money."

"How long had it been going on?"

"Quite a while. Right around the time of the Oak Glen incident, Trevor's partner was killed in the cross fire of a shoot-out with a couple of runners connected to the Mancuso family. While losing any agent in the line of duty is a tragedy, at the time I was too wrapped up in what I'd been through to pay much attention. Besides, we know the risks of the job, right? Looking back though, I'm not so sure it was an accident."

Blake frowned. "You think it was a hit?"

She nodded. "I'm about as sure as I can be. Now. Too bad no one could prove it."

"How did you find out Greenwood was on the take?"

"By sheer accident. The signs were all there, but I didn't see them." She shrugged. "Maybe I didn't want to see them. I had it bad for him. Like an idiot, I thought he was the one, so it was so easy to overlook a lot of things I shouldn't have. Like his apartment for one. He had this awesome place in the Village, way too nice for an agent's salary. When I asked him how he could afford it, he told me he'd gotten a sweet deal on a rent-controlled sublet. But then I saw a mortgage statement lying on the counter one night, the kind that gives you all the account information, balance, next payment due, principal and interest paid, that sort of thing. The principal paid was astronomical."

"No wonder you asked me about my place. How'd he explain it?"

"He fed me some line about it being his parents' place. They were supposedly retired and traveling the country in a Winnebago and he had power of attorney. He said he'd lied because he didn't think I'd be impressed with a guy that still technically lived at home with his parents."

"And you fell for this?" he asked incredulously.

"I told you. I *wanted* to believe him."

Who was he to pass judgment? Hadn't he been equally duped? No one had known Officer Kate Morgan had turned. They'd nearly lost an officer in the line of duty along with an innocent woman they were using as a decoy to draw out Devlin Shore, who was once connected with Clark. The same woman Blake's former partner, Mason, had fallen in love with and had nearly lost when they realized too late she'd been taken by Shore, with the assistance of Officer Morgan. But Bailey Grayson had been smart, and managed to get word to them about her location. They'd arrived in time, and other than a bullet to the leg, Bailey and the other girls Shore had kidnapped were safe. Mason and Bailey married and moved to Chicago to be near Mason's son, Cody. Last he'd heard, Bailey had just given birth to their third child, another girl.

So yeah, he knew what it was like, and a more bitter pill he'd never swallowed. "When did you finally catch on?"

"Not too much later," she said. "There were other signs, too. He had paintings, but claimed they were cheap starving-artist reproductions he'd picked up for a few bucks. After CSI and IA were through, it turned out those paintings alone were a nice chunk of change. There was a Jag he said belonged to his folks, but I later discovered it was registered in his name, and there was no lien holder on the paper, either.

"We were at his place after a bust. It was a big one for Trevor and he wanted to celebrate. When he disappeared into the bedroom and didn't come back right away, I thought..." She cleared her throat and shifted her gaze to the tapestry bedspread. "I thought he was busy making the room more romantic. After a couple of minutes I went down the hall and found him. He'd just opened a safe he kept in the bedroom and I'd thought he was putting his service revolver away, but he still had it holstered, which didn't make sense to me because I'd always seen him take it off before putting it away. That's when I saw the black canvas bag. Trevor had a similar bag, but his was leather, not canvas."

She traced a pattern on the bedspread with the tip of her finger. "He never saw me, but through the crack in the door I watched him transfer cash from the bag into the safe and put it next to the stacks of bills that were already there.

"I snuck back down the hall and called out to him that I was leaving. I came up with some lame excuse and got the hell out of there. I took the weekend off and avoided him as long as I could while I tried to figure out what to do, but because he was my partner, it wasn't that easy. Monday morning I told him that it wasn't going to work out between us and we should start dating other people."

"That must've gone over well."

A wry grin tugged her lips. "Like a lead balloon. But, I'd already requested a transfer, and I refused to talk to him about it. Where I really screwed up was not going to someone right away with what I suspected. I couldn't go to my father, because Trevor was like a second son to him. He was already having visions of the next generation of DEA agents."

He didn't miss the heavy sarcasm in her voice, but he knew enough about her to know she used it to mask the pain and disappointment.

"Besides," she said, shifting her attention back to him, "I felt like I needed more evidence before I openly accused Trevor. By all appearances, he was a good agent. His busts were clean, he was well liked. Plus, everyone knew we were having an affair, and the rumors had already started that Trevor dumped me and he was the one who'd requested the transfer. If I'd gone to anyone then, it would've looked like I was trying to get back at him for ending our relationship."

He wanted to hold her, to whisper words of comfort, but sensed she needed to get everything out in the open. According to McCall, she'd never talked to anyone about the incidents that had taken place. Letting her talk it out was probably the best thing he could do for her.

"Basically, I was pretty much screwed," she continued, "unless I somehow managed to bring Trevor down. I started tailing him when I wasn't on duty. For about two weeks there was nothing, then finally I got lucky. He was meeting with someone, and from the looks of the shiny black Lincoln parked outside a strip mall under construction I'd followed him to, I was pretty sure I was onto something.

"What I didn't know is that they'd be waiting for me. Somehow Trevor knew I'd been tailing him, and I walked right into a trap set by him and Johnny Mancuso. Mancuso was a connected guy," she said, then waited for him to acknowledge he understood her meaning. As in connected to the mob.

"They planned to kill me and make it look like I was the one on the take. Trevor would be the conquering hero once again, and while it'd be a tragedy that another agent was killed, it'd be understandable considering the type of people I was really working for."

The twisting in his gut no longer took him by surprise, nor did the fierce desire to protect her, not just from the bad guys, but from herself. She had more determination and sheer will than any woman he'd ever known. More than some cops he knew, too.

She shifted on the bed and stretched her legs out in front of her. After leaning back on her hands, she shook her head, her expression one of self-deprecation. "You know, I really thought that was it, but someone was obviously looking out for me. Trevor and Mancuso started arguing and I took advantage of it by charging Mancuso. He managed to fire off a shot and thankfully missed. We both went down. Mancuso was pierced by a piece of rebar sticking out of the floor." She pulled in a shaky breath and let it out slow. "I grabbed his gun and..."

"Shot Greenwood," he finished for her.

Ronnie closed her eyes and struggled to breathe evenly as the pain washed over her in hard, crashing waves. No longer was it the pain of Trevor's betrayal that haunted her. The pain came from another source, one much closer to her heart that no matter how hard she tried, she just couldn't put behind her.

She opened her eyes and looked at Blake, trying to take comfort from the compassion and caring banked in his silvery gaze, but it'd been so long she wasn't sure she knew how. But no one, not even the man she cared about deeply could lessen the pain of a father's angry words of betrayal.

Blake moved onto the bed and arranged the thick feather pillows behind him against the headboard. He reached out for her and she hesitated for only a second. She curled into him, loving the feel of his arms holding her, if only for a while longer. They only had a few hours at the most until they'd begin the laborious task of wrapping up the case, and eventually saying goodbye.

The thought of leaving filled her with a different kind of anguish, the kind that tore at her heart with sharp claws. The kind that threatened her to the point she feared she'd never recover.

"It was kill or be killed," she told him. "I had no other choice."

His arms around her tightened. "I know you didn't, sweetheart."

"I've never talked about it, and that's made it a lot worse for me. Not even my father knows the entire story, although it wasn't because I never tried to talk to him. He sees things his way, and there's nothing I can do about it unless he's willing to meet me halfway and at least listen. Only the investigating officials from IA and the crime lab and, of course, my immediate superiors know what really took place. I was prepared to leave the agency then, because I knew the guys in my unit would make my life a living hell, and they have. None of them wanted to be partnered with me, and I can't blame them. So they put me with a rookie transfer, someone who hadn't heard all the bullshit, and that's where I've been until now.

"When I heard about the bonus on this case, I volunteered. I thought I'd do my job, collect the extra pay and leave the agency behind, and for once, not have to put up with all the innuendo and doubt. But it didn't work that way, thanks to Scott. I never wanted any of this. I've had enough."

He smoothed his hand up her hip, his fingers coming to rest at her waist where his fingers toyed with the hem of her blouse. "I understand why you'd want to leave the agency," he said, "but an antique store?"

She tilted her head back until she could see his eyes. Compassion, caring and another more complex emotion shone in his silvery gaze. The same complexity she feared was reflected in her own. She wasn't sure how or when, but the sparks of awareness that led to the inevitable passion neither one of them had been able to prevent had grown into something much deeper. Love? She supposed it could be, not that she was any great expert on the subject. All she did know was that from the moment she'd first met him, he'd gotten under her skin and managed to climb all the way into her heart. Which made leaving all the more difficult.

"My mother's family lives in Savannah. It's far enough away from my parents in New York, but still close enough that I'll see them occasionally when they come to visit my grandparents. I want a quiet life, Blake. No more chasing bad guys. No more guns. No more gossip."

A slight smile curved his mouth. "I just don't see it, sweetheart. You'll be bored inside of a month."

"I have an MBA and a degree in criminal justice. Going into business for myself just makes sense."

He chuckled and shook his head. "Then you're really going to go stir-crazy. Have you given any thought to joining Corporate America?"

She smiled and moved so she was straddling his lean hips. "I want to wake up every morning and know that what I'm doing isn't going to revolve around life or death decisions. No one is going to come gunning for me if I don't have a display case dusted." She'd made her decision and nothing he, or anyone else for that matter, said was going to change her mind.

"You're taking the easy way out," he said. "You can't hide from the world, Ronnie. That's not a life, that's hibernation."

Her smile faded as she smoothed her hands up his chest and over his shoulders to clasp them behind his neck. "We don't have much time," she said before placing a light kiss on his lips. "Let's not spend what we have left in a discussion that will go nowhere."

His hands gripped her hips. He pulled her tight against him, and the ridge of his penis pulsed against her through the heavy denim. The answering call of her body was instantaneous with a sharp tug of desire.

"It doesn't have to—"

She placed her finger over his lips to still his argument. "Shh," she whispered, not wanting to hear that it didn't have to be goodbye. Goodbye was her only option. She was already in too deep. If she left now, she still had a chance of keeping her heart intact. Walking away would by far be the toughest thing she'd ever done, but it was better than leaving herself open for total heartbreak later. "I don't want to talk anymore, Blake. Just make love to me."

13

DESIRE MAY HAVE darkened Blake's eyes, but she knew he had an argument or two hovering on his tongue. She didn't want arguments. She didn't want to think about the future, or the past, she only wanted to feel his body aligned with hers, to have him deep inside her, loving her one last time.

"I want to make you promises," he said, running his hand down her back in a long sweeping motion.

"I know," she said quietly. She touched his hair and let the short strands sift through her fingers. "But all I have is now. It's all I can give."

He gently cupped her face in his hands, carefully rubbing his thumb over her lips. She pulled in a deep breath and closed her eyes, taking in the scents and textures that were uniquely Blake, cataloging them with painstaking care to retrieve later. He lowered his head and coaxed her lips to part with his, teasing her with his tongue, then sweeping inside to taste her.

Their lips still joined, he rolled her over to her back and started undressing her. Her skin sizzled where he touched. Oh, how she needed him to soothe the ache of sweet anticipation.

Frantic to feel the full length of his body pressed against hers, she tugged his shirt free of his trousers and ran her hands over his torso. It didn't take them long to shed their clothes, and begin the journey into heaven.

She moaned softly and arched her hips toward him, pressing insistently against the hard length of him until she thought she'd come out of her skin if he didn't fill her soon.

"Impatient, are we?" he teased with a chuckle against her lips.

"I want you, Blake," she said, not at all surprised by the husky purr of her voice. He did that to her. Made her feel soft and sexy all at the same time. She nipped playfully at his lips, then soothed the spot with the tip of her tongue. "Now."

He ignored her demand and took his sweet time, building the tension with his expert hands and mouth. Exploring her body, he touched, tasted and carried her dangerously close to madness. She'd imagined their last time to be slow so they could savor every last second they had together, but it was not to be. Her touch became as persistent as his, her mouth equally demanding until she could no longer determine where her body ended and his began.

He slid over her with aching slowness, then caught her mouth in a deep, toe-curling kiss. As much as she'd protested against tomorrows, nothing in her life could have prepared her for the tender emotions that consumed her when she cradled him between her thighs this last time. She arched against him, and he slid deep within her.

He held her face in both hands, his thumbs tenderly

caressing her temples. "Let me love you, Ronnie," he whispered. "Trust me. Trust your heart."

Her eyes burned with unshed tears as she writhed against him, coaxing him deeper inside her body. Against her will, she felt herself falling into an emotional storm, her defenses stripped away by the love shining in his eyes. Without safeguards to protect her, the walls surrounding her heart crumbled and the battle was lost.

Defeat had never tasted so sweet.

He captured her hands, palm to palm, and laced their fingers together as their bodies met and parted in infinite rhythm until they were swept away on a thunderous wave of mutual climax.

As she lay beneath him, she understood that her heart now belonged to him. And God help her, she never wanted him to let go.

THE RINGING OF THE telephone jarred Blake from his peaceful slumber. "Yeah," he said into the mouthpiece. He checked his watch. It was nearly five in the afternoon, three hours since they'd returned to shore.

Ronnie stirred beside him, the warmth of her body curled against his side. He could get used to waking up like this, and hoped he could convince her of the same. Getting his hopes up wasn't smart, but after everything she'd told him, he wasn't about to let her go when fear was the only thing keeping them from being together. He'd conquer her fears, one at a time if necessary, until he had the complete and total surrender of her heart. Whether she realized it or not, she already held his in her hands.

"You're good to go, ol' buddy."

He was instantly awake at the sound of Luke's jovial voice. They were taking a risk in not using a secure line, especially if Ramsey's memory had kicked in and Clark was on to them. It'd be nothing for Clark to have their calls monitored by someone at the resort. But Luke understood the dangers, and Blake knew his partner would be careful about revealing too much.

"Your new best friend gave it up?" Blake asked, his voice gravelly from sleep. Ronnie sat up and looked at him, waiting.

"Like a goddamn canary." Luke laughed. "Wouldn't tell us squat though until we promised him a sweetheart deal and a little added protection."

Blake nodded to Ronnie and watched as she slipped from beneath the tangled sheets and headed into the bathroom. The sight of her delicious curves had his body stirring. Not for the first time he cursed the fact that reality intruded on their time together when he'd like nothing better than to pull her back into bed and love her again. Seconds later, sounds of running water from the shower drifted into the room. He wished there was time to join her.

"I have everything you're gonna need for this, uh...corporate takeover," Luke finally said. "Ready to rattle some cages, buddy?"

He thought of Clark, and what could've happened to Ronnie if he'd found her with the evidence she'd located. "I've never been more ready," he said with deadly calm.

The rustling of papers drifted over the phone line. "I'm ready to fax the paperwork. You're going to find all the details you need to start the...uh...to complete the takeover."

As soon as Luke faxed the warrants to the number McCall had given them, they'd let the Coast Guard know it was time to move.

Blake cleared his throat. "Doesn't seem right doing this one without the calvary." Once Mason O'Neill transferred to Chicago, Blake had been without a partner, until an arrogant greenhorn from patrol walked into the vice detective's squad and told him he could relax now because the cavalry had arrived. Considering he'd been up to his elbows in grunt work, Luke's timing couldn't have been better. They'd been friends and partners ever since.

"Just keep your back to the wall," Luke said with a chuckle. "Give 'em hell, buddy."

Blake had no doubt he would.

GEORGIA ANDERSON LOOKED like the star center of a women's basketball team. Reed thin and surprisingly muscular, the agent was savvy and had a dry sense of humor. Blake liked her immediately, and didn't sense any animosity coming from Georgia toward Ronnie as he did with McCall.

After Luke's call, there hadn't been time for Ronnie and him to talk, but Blake planned to rectify that once they had Clark safely behind bars.

They'd gone to meet McCall and Anderson in the small apartment they were sharing during their assigned duty at Seaport Manor. By the time he and Ronnie had arrived, the warrants from Luke were coming through the fax machine, along with a copy of the signed confession from Hillman, which filled in details Luke couldn't reveal during their brief conversation.

"Looks like I was right about the drugs being on the island," Blake said, taking the chair closest to Ronnie at the round table set in the dining area. He finished reading Hillman's confession and handed the documents to Ronnie. "There's an old abandoned WWII bunker near the cove, where Hillman claims they're manufacturing the stuff."

McCall spun a chair around and straddled it. "That still doesn't explain Clark's scheduled appearances," he said, "or how he's linked to the resort."

"Oh, he's connected to it all right," Blake said. "That bunker is on Seaport property, which, we've discovered, *is* owned by one of Clark's legitimate corporations."

"Can you confirm that?" Georgia asked. She slipped a 9 mm into her shoulder holster.

"My guess is Luke has LAPD's white-collar unit working on it as we speak."

"According to this," Ronnie said, flipping the page, "Clark not only owns the resort, but he's the one bringing in supplies to the lab. From what Hillman states here, Clark's yacht is a party boat. Most of the high rollers on board are legit, and they cover what he's really doing while cruising up and down the coast."

McCall nodded in agreement. "Makes sense to me. Who's going to question a bunch of fat cats playing on a big fancy boat?"

"No one," Blake agreed. "Half the shipment comes through San Pedro on the water taxis. The other half Clark carries with him down to Mexico, where it's smuggled in through Texas. He drops anchor here off the island by the cove."

"We're going to need some help on this one," Georgia said. "I suggest we contact the local DEA office."

Ronnie stood and shrugged into a thin black windbreaker with the letters DEA printed in large yellow letters on the back. "You can try, but I don't think there's time to cut through all the bureaucracy," she said. "Clark said he was pulling anchor tonight. We have to move now, Georgia."

"Any idea what time?" McCall asked.

"No," Blake answered. "He only arrived yesterday and already a shipment has hit the streets. Chances are he's got his cargo and is ready to set sail for Mexico."

"Maybe not."

They all looked at Ronnie expectantly. "I checked his books, remember? Nothing's recorded as being taken on board."

Georgia shook her head. "That doesn't mean anything, Carmichael. Maybe he's a lousy bookkeeper."

Ronnie pulled her badge out of the pocket of her jacket and slipped the chain around her neck. "Then we have to find that bunker. If the drugs have been moved, then we know they're aboard the *Mary Alice*."

Tiny lines bracketed Georgia's warm chocolate eyes when she flashed them all a confident grin. "And if they're not, then we secure the lab and wait for good ol' Alister to make his regularly scheduled appearance."

"What about local law enforcement?" Ronnie asked. "Shouldn't we use them to secure the resort?"

McCall shook his head and stood. "Not a good idea. We don't know if they're on Clark's payroll or not."

Blake stuffed the appropriate warrant in his pocket and stood, handing the rest of the faxed details to McCall. "You and Anderson rendezvous with the Coast Guard vessel to seize and board Clark's yacht. Ronnie and I will locate the lab since we've seen the cove."

Ronnie checked the clip of her pistol, then holstered her weapon. She gave him a direct look and a brisk nod. "Let's do it."

For once, she didn't spout her standard "this is a DEA operation" speech. Progress, he thought. Definite progress. How that translated on a personal level remained to be seen, but he planned to find out soon enough.

RONNIE EASED UP beside Blake, crawling on her belly to the edge of the steep bluff. Below lay the cove, and since their luck seemed to be holding, they found the *Mary Alice* still anchored about two hundred yards in the distance. She wasn't sure what she expected, a flurry of activity maybe, since they knew Clark planned to pull out soon, but it certainly wasn't the almost-eerie silence. At least they still had the element of surprise on their side, because if Clark had known they were coming, there was a high probability his people would be clearing the place out and destroying evidence.

The sun had already begun its descent in the west, making the interior of the cove difficult to see because of the waning light. "We need to go down," she said quietly. "We'll never find the entrance to the lab from up here."

Blake kept his attention on the area below them. "I don't suppose I could talk you into staying put while I go check it out."

"Don't count on it," she said as she rose into a crouched position. She didn't tell him that her determination had little to do with a masochistic desire to be where the action might take place, but an overpowering need not to let him out of her sight.

He let out a sigh and indicated toward the rear of the cove as he eased back from the ledge. "Let's double back. I think I see an easier way down over there."

The hair on the back of her neck tingled. Still balanced on the balls of her feet, she turned her head to look behind her. Blake moved quickly, too quickly. Then she heard a grunt and saw him crumble to the ground beside her.

It was the last thing she saw before her world went dark.

A STEADY DRONE, almost like a deep-throated throb, buzzed irritatingly in Ronnie's ears as she slowly regained consciousness. The repetitive sound only added to the fierce pounding in her head.

She opened her eyes, then immediately closed them when the pounding increased, sending more piercing pain through her skull. Whoever had knocked her cold had done a whopper of a job, because she was pretty sure she had concussion.

Where was she? And what had they done to Blake?

She pulled in a slow breath, and told herself not to panic so she could get her bearings and find a way out. At least they hadn't trussed her up like some prized rodeo calf.

With her eyes still closed against the pain, she concentrated on breathing evenly and let her senses go to work. As far as she could determine, wherever they'd taken her, she was alone. There were no sounds, nor did she have the sense that she was being watched. The monotonous droning she guessed to be a generator. The distant sound of rushing water wasn't as clear, but she sensed no movement, which meant she and Blake hadn't been taken aboard the ship. Beneath her, the surface was hard, cool and slightly damp, and there was zilch by way of air circulation, adding to the near-stifling humidity.

Slowly, she opened her eyes again, blinking against the dull glare from a single bulb high in the ceiling. Once she adjusted to the dull light, she surveyed her surroundings. Concluding they'd been taken inside the bunker, she guessed she was being held in an old holding cell or brig. A small window with bars across it served no purpose as it'd been sealed shut from the outside with brick.

A door opened, followed by the sound of voices, growing louder as they neared. The scrape of metal followed and the door to her cell swung open on rusty hinges.

She swallowed a gasp as Blake was dragged into the room and laid none too gently on the floor. The side of his head was caked in blood, and his lip was split and already swollen. Even in the dull light she could make out what was going to be a very nasty bruise on his left cheek. It took every ounce of willpower she possessed not to move instantly to his side and see for herself the extent of the injuries the bastards had inflicted upon him. If her jailers had no idea how important he was to her, then they couldn't use him as leverage.

So instead, she ignored his lifeless form and glared at Nick, the only one of her captors she recognized. She had a barrage of questions, but remained stoically silent. There was no guessing how much they knew, and she wasn't about to help them out by filling in the blanks. From the beating they'd given Blake, he obviously wasn't talking, either.

Nick's eyes were cold and leering. Not a single resemblance to the kindly elder gentleman who'd escorted them to the yacht earlier that day. "Enjoy your stay at lower Seaport Manor," he said with a chuckle, then ushered the younger man out the door.

She waited until she heard the click of the lock, followed by the distant sound of the other door closing before she bolted to Blake's side.

Using extreme care, she checked him for additional injuries. Finding none, she carefully lifted his head onto her lap. Her vision blurred from the tears burning her eyes and she choked back a sob. "God, you're a mess," she whispered around the lump lodged in her throat. "You'll be okay. You *have* to be okay. I couldn't stand it if anything happened to you."

He remained limp in her arms. The only sign of life came from the steady rise and fall of his chest. Careful not to jostle him too much, she hugged him to her and rocked slowly, back and forth, back and forth, for what felt like hours, and there was still no sign of him regaining consciousness.

"Please wake up, Blake. Dammit, wake up," she whispered. Her throat burned from the tears she was afraid to shed, and felt as raw as her emotions. She loved him. That was the only explanation for the horrific pain ripping through her at the thought of never seeing his silver eyes filling with desire again, or never hearing the laughter and gentleness in his voice, or feeling his love in every touch.

She looked down at him and cupped his bruised cheek in her palm. "I can't lose you," she whispered. "I need you. Is that what you want to hear? That I need you. That I love you. Because I do. I love you, Blake."

His eyes slowly opened and the sweetest, sexiest smile she'd ever seen spread over his face as he looked

up at her. "Tell me that last part again," he said grog-
gily.

She made an indignant sound and shoved him
away. His head hit the dirt floor with a *thunk* as she
scrambled to her feet.

"Ow," Blake muttered. He rubbed at the back of his
head, already throbbing from the butt of the gun used
to knock him unconscious, not once, but twice.

"You were listening the entire time," she accused.

"No," he groused, as he pushed himself off the
floor. "Just the part where you said you couldn't live
without me and you loved me."

"That was low, Blake. Very low," she said, her turquoise eyes glistening. "And I didn't say I couldn't
live without you."

He took a jagged step toward her, and pulled her
into his arms. "You said you needed me. And you
loved me."

"Oh, Blake, thank God you're alive." Her slender
arms wrapped around his middle and she held on
tight as she sobbed against him. "I don't know what I
would have done if they'd killed you."

He tightened his hold. "I was thinking pretty much
the same thing when they wouldn't let me see you."

He didn't know how long they stood like that, their
arms wrapped around each other in the middle of the
dirty, dank cell, but finally the flow of her tears ebbed.

"They didn't hurt you?" he asked, holding her so
tight she wiggled in his arms. He loosened his hold
slightly. If his head didn't feel as though it'd been slit

in two, he might have actually enjoyed that little wiggle of hers a whole lot more.

"No." She pulled back and swiped at the tears staining her cheeks. "What happened? What did they do to you?"

"Our cover was blown when Ramsey's memory kicked in. They figured we'd be back, so they set up surveillance all over the cove," he said.

"Why are we here? What are they planning to do with us?"

"My guess is they're going to leave us here to die, otherwise they would have taken us aboard ship. No one knows about this place and it could be months before anyone comes looking for us. Or so they think. Nick wasn't too forthcoming with details when I asked him." He managed a grin that caused his lip to bleed again. "But then neither was I."

She used her shirttail to dab at his lip. "Is that why they beat you?"

The pain in her voice tugged at his heart. "Nah. That was just for shits and giggles."

The look in her eye said she didn't believe him.

He sighed. "They wanted to know how many of us good guys are on the island," he admitted. "They think we're it."

"We have to find a way out of here," she said, and pulled out of his arms.

"Look around, sweetheart. There's only one way out of here and I don't think they left the key. McCall and Anderson know where we are. Once they board the yacht and don't find us, they'll know where to look."

She let out a sigh and moved back into his arms. "We're going to miss all the fun, you know."

He shrugged and kissed the edge of her mouth. Thanks to his busted lip, anything more adventurous would hurt like the devil. "That's okay. Although I would have liked to do it myself, I'll have to settle for imagining the look on the SOB's face when Anderson and McCall throw him down and cuff him."

A wicked smile curved her lips. "What do we do now?"

He chuckled, and his ribs hurt. "We wait for the cavalry to arrive while I tell you over and over again how much I love you."

She laughed, and the sound was sweeter than life. "Now there's a plan I can live with."

"So does this mean I can interest you in a beachfront condo?"

14

One Month Later

"HOW MUCH MORE you got stowed in that thing?" Blake asked, as he hefted another heavy box filled with Ronnie's belongings in his arms. No wonder she'd wanted to open a gift shop. He must've hauled a dozen cartons marked Fragile into the spare bedroom already.

She still hadn't made any career decisions, other than leaving the agency. During the last month she'd talked a lot about her options, and was toying with the idea of law school or perhaps teaching criminal justice at any one of the dozens of universities and state colleges in the area. Whatever she eventually decided, all he wanted was for her to be happy.

She pushed another large carton to the edge of the moving van. "At least a dozen or so more. You're the one who said not to hire movers." She planted her hands on her hips and laughed. "What's the matter, He-Man. You pooped already?"

She let out a squeal and another burst of laughter when he set the carton back on the truck and jumped inside with her. "Blake, we'll never finish this way. I'd like to have everything done before we leave for Hawaii so I don't have to deal with it when we come home."

He advanced on her, backing her up until she came to a stop when her bottom brushed against the mattress standing on end. Bracing his hands on either side of her, he trapped her within his arms and leaned close. "I think we should start a new project instead."

Desire darkened her eyes, eyes he'd never tire of gazing into, especially since they were now openly filled with love. For him.

She hadn't agreed to marry him. Yet. Moving in together was a big step for her, but he was more than willing to be patient when it came to putting a ring on her finger. He figured it was only a matter of time anyway before he convinced her.

They hadn't spent more than a few hours down in the bunker thanks to Georgia's stellar interrogation skills on Nick. Ramsey, they'd later determined, wasn't as involved with Clark as they'd originally believed, but he had been removed from the bench when it was learned he'd accepted bribe money to allow a few criminals to walk. Billy Hillman had been placed in the witness protection program until Clark's trial, and they'd heard that Clark's wife had filed for divorce.

With Clark and most of his crew safely behind bars awaiting trial, there was a little less coke being sold on the streets. At least until the next Alister Clark arrived on the scene.

He pushed against the mattress with his hands and wiggled his eyebrows at her. "Hmm. Soft."

She slipped her hands beneath his shirt and

smoothed them over his skin. He'd never get bored of her touch. "Someone could walk by and see us."

He dipped his head and nibbled on her earlobe. "Danger's supposed to make sex even hotter." She moaned softly when he traced the shell of her ear with his tongue.

She let out a sexy little sigh that had his erection straining painfully against the fly of his jeans. "You mean it can get hotter?"

She looped her hands around his neck and he lifted her into his arms. He carried her out of the back of the moving van and up the stairs to the condo and maneuvered them inside.

"Where are we going?" she asked, nuzzling his neck.

"I'm taking you under the covers, baby, where it's gonna get a whole lot hotter." And that's where he planned to keep her for the rest of their lives.

CALL THE ONES YOU LOVE OVER THE HOLIDAYS!

Save $25 off future book purchases when you buy any four Harlequin® or Silhouette® books in October, November and December 2001,

PLUS

receive a phone card good for 15 minutes of long-distance calls to anyone you want in North America!

WHAT AN INCREDIBLE DEAL!

Just fill out this form and attach 4 proofs of purchase (cash register receipts) from October, November and December 2001 books, and Harlequin Books will send you a coupon booklet worth a total savings of $25 off future purchases of Harlequin® and Silhouette® books, AND a 15-minute phone card to call the ones you love, anywhere in North America.

Please send this form, along with your cash register receipts as proofs of purchase, to:
In the USA: Harlequin Books, P.O. Box 9057, Buffalo, NY 14269-9057
In Canada: Harlequin Books, P.O. Box 622, Fort Erie, Ontario L2A 5X3
Cash register receipts must be dated no later than December 31, 2001.
Limit of 1 coupon booklet and phone card per household.
Please allow 4-6 weeks for delivery.

**I accept your offer! Enclosed are 4 proofs of purchase.
Please send me my coupon booklet
and a 15-minute phone card:**

Name: _____

Address: _____ City: _____

State/Prov.: _____ Zip/Postal Code: _____

Account Number (if available): _____

---

097 KJB DAGL
PHQ4013

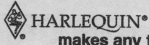

Look to the stars
for love and romance
with bestselling authors

JUDITH ARNOLD
KATE HOFFMANN
and GINA WILKINS

in

WRITTEN
IN THE
STARS

Experience the joy of
three women who dare to
make their wishes for love
and happiness come true in
this *brand-new* collection
from Harlequin!

Available in December 2001
at your favorite retail outlet.

HARLEQUIN®
Makes any time special ®

Visit us at www.eHarlequin.com   PHWS

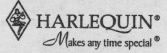